I0519496

Step Into Darkness

By

LEX MARIE

Step Into Darkness

Published By

Bellevue Publishers

www.BellevuePublishers.com

Introduction

MY NAME IS LEX MARIE, I AM 30 YEARS OLD AND A MOTHER. I AM NEW TO WRITING BOOKS, THOUGH I HAVE ALWAYS ENJOYED WRITING. I ENJOYING READING AND SPENDING TIME WITH MY FAMILY.

Description

LAYLA, IS FRESH OUT OF HIGH SCHOOL AND HEADED MILES FROM HOME TO START COLLEGE. OUT TO DO WHAT MAKES HER HAPPY AGAINST HER FATHER'S WISHES. LAYLA, GETTING A SCHOLARSHIP AND FULL RIDE IS ABLE TO BREAK FREE FROM HER FATHERS GRASP. LAYLA IS AN OLD SOUL AND VALUES LOVE AND CONNECTION FROM PEOPLE AROUND HER ESPECIALLY WHEN IT COMES TO DATING. UNFORTUNATELY LIFE DOESN'T GO THE WAY SHE PLANNED. WHEN SHE TELLS A PUNK FRAT BOY NO, SHE ENDS UP KICKED OUT OF COLLEGE AND HOMELESS. REBUILDING HER LIFE HAS BEEN HARD BUT SHE MADE IT WORK. UNTIL AN EX-BOYFRIEND'S EGO TURNS INTO AN USAFE SITUATION FOR LAYLA. SHE FINDS HERSELF WITH A VIOLENT STALKER. WHILE NOT EXPECTING IT, LAYLA FINDS HERSELF IN THE PRESENCE OF THE MYSTERIOUS CAMERON MAGNOLLIA. THE SPARKS ARE UNDENIABLE BETWEEN THE TWO. COULD MEETING AND FALLING FOR CAMERON MAGNOLIA, THE CEO OF MAGNOLIA METAL WORKS SAVE HER LIFE? OR WILL LIFE KEEP RAPIDLY UNRAVELING AROUND THEM?

Chapter 1

LAYLA

"I can't do this anymore." I say to myself. I am living on campus, trying to get my bachelor's in architecture. I was lucky to get a full-ride scholarship. But I did my best in school, knowing I didn't want to stay in my home town forever. I grew up in a small town in Arkansas. My dad owned his own construction company. He had been trying to groom me my whole life to take over for him. I didn't want that life, though. I love the architecture of buildings and how they are made. But I never wanted to run the company. Business just wasn't for me. He never understood why I couldn't just be happy doing what he was doing. My mom, she was more understanding. She wanted me to chase my dreams and be the best version of my self. I know it sounds cliché, but she really was my best friend. Unfortunately, life ended early for her. She battled hard against the cancer that plagued her mind. But in the end, it wasn't enough. That was my junior year of high school when I lost my best friend. My dad became more of an asshole if that is even possible. He took to drinking after my mom passed. Life for me got a lot harder, and my dad was verbally abusive on a normal day, but drunk was way worse. He never hit me; that's about the only thing he had going for him. After focusing and studying hard my whole senior year, I got my scholarship! I was so excited. I got accepted into The University of Nevada! I tried to explain to my dad that I would be leaving and going there to study architecture. Needless to say, it didn't go over well. He was furious, told me if I left ,never come back because I wouldn't be welcome. The next day, while he was passed out drunk. I packed my bags, threw them in my crappy old car, and drove away from everything I had ever known with tears running down my face.

As I sit here in my college dorm with all my bags packed, I think about what on earth I am going to do now. While here, I had to work 2 part-time jobs, plus my studies. I started talking to someone while working at one of my part-time jobs. He was nice and seemed to like me. A couple of weeks into hanging out, he got pissed because I wouldn't sleep with him. I didn't understand why he was so mad. He could have just broken up with me and dated someone else. But I fucked up in not knowing who he was. Apparently, he was the Dean's son, and that completely screwed me. He made up a bunch of lies and fed them to his dad, who then kicked me out of his college. So, that's great. I stand from my bed and wipe my tears one last time. I grab my bags and head down to my car. I managed to make it through 2 whole semesters here without even being noticed. Now I'm being kicked out all because I wouldn't have sex with the Dean's son. How fucking pathetic! As I drive out of the college parking lot, I don't even look back. I drive to the opposite side of town, which is about 30 min drive. I find a hotel that doesn't look super run down. Luckily, working 2 jobs has been helpful in setting back some money. I get a room and take my bags inside because, at this point, I have no idea how long I'm going to have to be here. Pulling myself together, I decided to take a shower and wash away the bullshit. Once out, I throw on sweats and grab my phone. I start searching for apartments. Which seems to be way more expensive then I was hoping for. I would have to quit my 2 part times and get a real full-time job to handle these payments. I feel ill just thinking about it. I decide to take a nap and start again later.

3 Years Later

LAYLA

Just another great day in the life of a 23-year-old loser. I swear I was meant for more than this. But instead, I get up every day and get myself around for work. Just another dead-end job. It pays my bills and keeps food on my table, so even though I hate it, I still find myself going. I live by myself in a little corner flat, it's nothing fancy, but it's only 10 minutes from work. Plus, a bonus is the little mom-and-pop coffee place right down the road; they make a killer caramel frappe! I want to do so much more with my life. I feel like I am meant for something big! I just don't know where to go or how to get there. Unfortunately, I have had several bad relationships where I am looking for things in all the wrong places. Hints why they never seem to last, and I'm always swearing off men. You know, like it's going to last more than a couple of months. It never lasts, though big surprise there, and so here I am, still hoping that someday I will find that perfect guy for me. The ones you read about who love you for you and not what they can get from you.

It is Friday, though, so I guess that is something to look forward to. I woke up with a text from my best friend Leah this morning. I swear she and I are one and the same and will get our lives together someday!

Leah,

Lay, I'm running late. Can you stop for breakfast and coffee this morning?!

Layla,

Of course! But you owe me Monday!!

I just have to focus on getting through today, and then I can come back home and continue to wallow in my own self-pity.

As soon as I walked into work, Leah was there waiting for me. I may complain about my life, but I seriously have the best friend! We chatted for a few minutes before we headed out to our area to start working. As we walked, I saw several of our other co-workers already at their stations and making everything look nice and in order. I mean, yeah it needs to be done, but everyone getting to their stations early to do it is odd. I glance over at Leah, who gives me a knowing look. Once we got to our station, I broke and asked her why everyone was so on edge. Keep in mind that we work in a factory, so not much in this line of work should have people shake like this except for maybe an audit. But normally we have at least a week's notice before those to prepare. Our factory produces large metal ingots, and it's nothing fancy. Far from it, I go home every night covered from head to toe in dirt and grime, not to mention sweat, because it just so happens to be hotter than Haiti in this place. After a long pause, Leah finally informs me, "We are having a walk-through today by an important client. I guess if it doesn't go well, we could lose our contract with them, causing several job losses and possibly even a closure of the plant itself."

That catches my attention because I don't remember hearing anything about this. I, like everyone else, it seems, am stunned by this news. But honestly, it makes me wonder if something has happened that we out here as peons just weren't made aware of, and they decided to just drop last minute that they were going to make a surprise visit today. The problem is, no one told any of us what they were coming for or when. "We have no idea who from the company is even coming.

Though I doubt it will be the CEO" Leah gossips. "Magnolia Metal Works CEO Cameron Magnolia has rarely been seen out in public. I highly doubt he is going to take time out of his day to come down here just to do a walk-through." Leah sounds pretty sure of herself. But she isn't wrong; Cameron Magnolia is a very private person. No one knows much about him; it's hard even to find a picture of him. I personally have no idea what the guy even looks like. All we do know about him is that he took over the company from his parents after his brother and father died to help his mom. No one knows how they died, and it was very hush-hush, and kept out of the media for the most part. However, that was five years ago now. The only question I currently have is why are they coming here, and why on such short notice?

The lack of supervision in this plant alone should be enough to close this place down. It's no wonder the company that pretty much funds our entire facility wants to do a walk-through. But let's be real: if they have employees on the floor and are making a quota, that's all the management cares about. "Ugh, Leah you're sure we have no idea when or why?" I question her. "Like, what is the point of you being the center of the gossip train and my best friend if you can't give me the tea!" I glanced over at her, and we both just busted out laughing. She grins and side-eyes me before whispering, "I just found out this morning when I got here, and no one is willing to talk about it; they all seem genuinely spooked about it." I let it drop and got to work. Around 11:30, we decided to stop our machines and get ready to head up to the break room for lunch. We started chatting about possibly having a girl's night this weekend, maybe going to a local club and having a few drinks. Both Leah and I are single, as I have sworn off guys for the millionth time, and Leah just got out of a bad breakup about a month ago. We both have been so busy lately with overtime and well, life in general, that we haven't had a whole lot of time to get together and just hang out.

We are walking up to the break room, and I am listening to Leah talk about a potential club we could go to. When I glanced into the office, we were passing on the main walking path. There is a gentleman sitting at the end of the large oak table, he looks angry but composed. He seems to look as though he is paying attention to our plant manager, but I can tell his mind is elsewhere. I must have been standing and staring because he lookedover,, and we made eye contact. I can't read his expression; his face seems as though it has softened because he doesn't look as angry as when I first walked up. Leah grabs my arm, breaking my eye contact with this strange man, I look up to see a worried expression on her face. Trying to figure out why, I lock eyes with our plant manager, who is looking at us with a very scornful look on his face. We start to walk off just as he closes the blinds to the office. Leah is now looking at me like I have lost my mind, and honestly, she might be right. I am pretty sure my face is as red, considering how hot I feel. I am absolutely mortified; not only did I get caught staring by whoever that guy was in that meeting, but also my plant manager! Good grief, I swear I am getting fired!

Chapter 2

LAYLA

Leah and I walked the rest of the way to the break room quietly. Which is fine by me as I am doing my best to cool down from my mortifying moment. We grab our stuff and head over to our usual lunch table. It is at the far end of the room by one of the large windows. Leah just stares at me, waiting for an explanation I can only assume. But to be honest, I do not know what happened either. I glanced over, and when I saw him, something about the guy just drew me in. I could not figure out why or what it was. However, I had this overwhelming sensation, one I had never had before. I was attempting to identify the feeling, and during that period, I was working on understanding it, was when they all caught me staring. "Ugh." I groan at her stare. "Spill it!" Leah demands. "There is not anything to spill. Honestly, I am just as confused as you are about what happened. I am probably still tired and spaced out at the wrong time." I told her. She looks very unconvinced and stares at me for a few moments longer as if to try to look through my bullshit and straight to my core. I finally sigh and shrug at her, and luckily, she drops it for now. I know it will not be the last I hear about it, but I am grateful she has backed off. I already feel like such a creep, and being nagged about it all of lunch would have been torcher.

Lunch went by quickly, considering my mind was all over the place. I just could not seem to get that guy's face out of my head. I seem to be struggling with the weird feeling I had and what caused it. Was it the guy in the office, or was I just tired and spaced out at a bad time? Leah did not say anything for the rest of lunch, but amid my internal struggles, I saw her steal glimpses at me here and there. I

tried to smile like I was fine, though I was unsure if my smile looked real or not. Once we were heading back to our area from lunch, Leah and I picked up our conversation from earlier and tried to plan for our girls' night. As we walked and talked, I glanced over at the same office and noticed the blinds were still closed. I say a silent prayer for not being able to make a complete fool of myself again. We near our line and finalize our plans for girls' night out shenanigans tomorrow evening at Club Underground, which is right downtown.

We get back to work, and I am struggling to stay focused. I am excited about our girl's night tomorrow! I have never been to the club before; honestly, I do not even go out much. I am a huge homebody. But getting to just hang out with Leah and cut loose a little has me excited, especially after what happened today. I hear some commotion and glance at the clock, realizing I have been mindlessly working and lost in my thoughts for a few hours. I mean, I will not complain about the time passing quickly; however, I do notice how tense everyone is around me. As we wait to see the large group of people round the corner to our machines, I can only assume that they will be critiquing how we do our jobs and the efficiency of it all. When they do round the corner, the first person I see, Jeff, our plant manager, is looking right at me with probably the sharpest look I have ever received from anyone in my whole life. Which is saying a lot. So instinctually, I look straight down and start focusing a little too hard on what I am doing in front of me. I do not look up until I do not hear *anyone chatting in our area anymore and feel safe again. I peek up at Leah and notice her wide eyes as she stares at something behind me. I whip around and almost run straight into the man I was caught staring at earlier. Panic rises as he just stares at me intently with an unreadable expression. He must have been quiet this whole time, and I did not realize he had not moved on yet. He holds something out to me; I glance to see it is a piece of paper. I am still shocked as he puts the paper in my hand and then turns and saunters off like nothing happened. I am standing there stunned and frozen in place for a moment. I finally pulled myself out of my daze and stole a look at Leah, knowing she witnessed that also; she was just standing there with a questioning gaze and an eyebrow lifted, likely waiting for some kind of explanation again. Instead, I blew out the breath I did not realize I was holding and shoved that paper into my pocket. Do I want to know what that paper says? Um, absolutely, I do! However, I have way too many nosey Nancy's around me right now for me to read it. So, I get back to work, and the last hour of work drags on as I anticipate what that piece of paper could say.*

Finally, I am free from work and have the next 3 days off! When I stepped out of the building, I could still see several fancy cars in the front parking lot with the other office employees. I managed to make it to my car faster than I ever had before. I sat there for a while, trying to calm my nerves to read this paper. I am severely nervous; I feel like I might throw up! My anxiety is through the roof. First off, I have no idea who this guy is and what he has to do with the Magnolia Metal Works company. Nor do I know what he wants. Oh, my goodness, he probably hates being stared at, and I'm now in a bunch of shit for getting caught staring! I am such an idiot and feel like I might pass out! But, at the same time, the guy was the definition of gorgeous, so I would think that he is used to being stared at. Good grief, I need to get my anxiety under control! The only way to know what this guy wants is to just stop being such a pussy and read the damn paper! So, here goes nothing...

I don't know who you are or why you were staring at me. However, I would like to talk to you and maybe get some answers on some things. Please meet me at Club Underground at 9 pm tomorrow evening.

-C

Well, he does not seem angry, so that is good, at least. He seems just as confused as I am; Hm, I wonder if he felt the weird sensation also. Ah shit! He wants to talk to me. I wonder what it is he wants answers to. Maybe it is just work-related. I mean, Leah and I already had plans to go to Club Underground, but not until 11 pm. He asked me there 2 hours earlier, and I do not know that showing up alone in a nightclub to meet a guy you do not know seems like the smartest thing to do. I could just tell Leah about it and have her go with me. However, she is the gossip queen, and not knowing who this guy is, I am not really trying to make this a public situation. Now that I am all worked up, the only thing I can do is go home and try to relax. So first, I will order pizza and pick it up on my way home. Then eat it while I take a nice hot bath! Yeah, that sounds nice!

Cameron

I absolutely hate the fact that I had to come and do the walk-through of this plant today. It has nothing to do with the plant itself; I just have plenty of other meetings and business deals that I need to attend to. Yet the contract with this plant is about to expire soon. So, I had to come today to decide if we are going to re-sign or just let it expire and move forward. Not that this company is much use to mine, but our funding pretty much keeps it up and running. This company is neither hurting nor helping us. So, I am on the fence about what to do with it, if I am being honest. However, my father made this contract before he died, and I am not sure why, but I feel like I would be letting him down if I were to cut ties with this company. He seemed to have faith in it for reasons unknown to me. Ugh, it is hard to believe that it has been five years since they have passed. God, I miss them both so much! My poor mother has been through so much! Bless her heart, though, and she is always going out of her way to make sure everything is going well with me whenever she has the chance.

I should stay on topic; this poor plant manager is really doing his best here. Jeff, I think, that is what he said his name was. He is trying hard to give me some great reasons why I should renew our contract with them. I feel terrible, but I cannot seem to stay focused on him and what he is trying to present to us. I just want to tell him to hurry the fuck up, and I have more important things to attend to today than this. Though, if my mother heard that I dealt with this in such a manner, she would probably skin me alive. I am just starting to focus back on what Jeff is telling us when I start to feel this weird tingling sensation. *It is an odd feeling, and I also feel as though I am being watched, so I glance over to the exposed window that overlooks their shop floor. Standing in the window is a woman covered from head to toe in dirt. I am unsure what the weird tingling feeling is. However, I can deduce that even being covered in filth, the young woman is gorgeous. She broke our eye contact suddenly, and that is when I noticed the girl next to her. They are both now looking at their plant manager, Jeff, who is looking at them in a not-so-great manner. They start to scurry off to wherever they are headed as he shuts the blinds to the conference room.*

After that, he goes back to his proposal as if nothing has happened. I continue to watch him as he talks, trying to keep it looking as though I am paying attention because, at this point, I am far from hearing anything he is saying now. It's good that others from the company are here and paying attention to his proposal because I am officially out of touch with anything he is saying, and they can fill me in later. About another hour goes by, and I am anxious to get out of this conference room. Finally, he seems to be done with what he wants to say here. So, we got all our safety gear on and headed out to tour the floor. I am excited to see how this facility has progressed with the funds that we have provided over the last 5 years. During the time he was talking, I was still fixated on the woman in the window. I feel such a need to know her. I started writing a note to give her when I saw her out on the floor; I am hoping he just thinks that I was taking notes while he was talking. I need to know more about this girl and what that tingling feeling was. Such an odd sensation, but it also makes me wonder if she felt it too, and that is why she had stopped and stared to begin with. I am walking with everyone through the plant, though my head is still in a fog of curiosity from earlier in the day. We pause slightly, and I glance up to see the plant manager Jeff, giving the girl from earlier a pointed look. She does not even attempt *to look anywhere else; the girl drops her head and tries to stay focused on the task in front of her, trying not to get into any more trouble with her boss. But this will not do. I need to find a way to get this note to her. I try to hang back from the group a bit, and when she thinks everyone has left the area, she visibly relaxes and looks over to the girl she was walking with earlier. The girl is just staring at me with wide eyes, causing my mystery girl to whirl around and almost run straight into me. With her so close, I wondered what her skin would feel like, clean from all this dirt. I also want to just reach out and pull her to me, and we are so close it would not take much. But once I meet her gaze, I can see in her eyes that she is curious but also afraid. Her eyes widened, and I did not wish to get her into more trouble. So I slip the note into her hand and turn on my heels to get back to the group, hoping no one notices I am missing. Luckily, it does not seem anyone has noticed, or if they did, no one is saying anything about it. So, I am quiet and follow everyone else through the rest of the facility tour.*

Chapter 3

LAYLA

⁓

I am so conflicted! It is 6 pm, and I am running out of time to make my decision! Either I go and chance being murdered or kidnapped by this guy I do not know, or wait and go later with Leah. But what if I wait and go later, and he is still there waiting for me, and then he will know that I intentionally blew him off! Oh my gosh, I am panicking! I need another hot bath! About 2 hours later, I am finally climbing out of the bath and drying off when I hear my phone ping. I dry my hands and check my texts to see it from Leah.

Leah,

Hey Bish, are we good to meet at 9 instead of 11? I forgot that I have plans in the morning with my mom, and I swear if I flake on her again, she is going to kill me!

Well, I guess she just made up my mind for me. I am not thrilled, but maybe I can pretend I forgot about meeting with him. Yeah, that is what I will stick with if he tries to approach me.

Layla,

That is fine; I do not feel like being out till early morning tonight anyway.

So now all that is left is to figure out what I am going to wear and how I should do my hair. Unfortunately, I have around an hour to figure it out. Let us be real: I am not going out for anything except to have a good time tonight. So, I just decided to go with something simple. We got some ass-hugging jeans and my favorite off-the-shoulder crop top. I put some quick curls in my hair and pinned half of it up, with some light makeup to finish off my look. I am not there to impress anyone tonight, I mean, unless I do end up running into my mystery guy, then maybe a little.

Cameron

I am sitting in the Club Underground in a far back booth, trying not to draw attention to myself. Luckily for me, this place is dark on the inside, aside from the colored strobe lights. I have to say though, I am damn nervous. I never go out, and this is the last place I want to be right now. Not that I cannot go out and have a good time; I am just uncomfortable in large crowds of people, so I just never really have any interest in being out. But I asked my mystery girl from yesterday here, and I would feel like a huge asshole if she did end up showing up and I did not. As I sit here waiting, I keep getting curious glances from several other women. Some look like they want to approach me and say something; others look like they might just pounce on me. Do not get me wrong, I know that I am a good-looking guy. I could really have whatever girl I want when I want. They just do not interest me;

I have way too many things going on in the company that keep me busy, and I just do not have time for all the extra mess that comes with being in a relationship. Not to mention, most women just want me for my money and what they can get from me, not who I am as a person, and that is one of the worst feelings.

I checked my watch and realized it was 9:30, and she must not have been as intrigued by me as I was with her. I decided to stay a little while longer, and people-watch for a bit since I do not get out much. I scan the crowd of people on the dance floor, bodies grinding on each other like they have no care in the world. I stop short when I glance over at the bar. The ass on the woman across the room is the sexiest thing I have seen, and for the first time in what feels like forever, I am rock hard, and I have only seen this girls' ass. I can assume she has her back to me getting a drink. I swear those are the kind of pants that would have any man standing at attention in an instant. Hell, I am, and I rarely take an interest in any woman. With her back to me, I can take in all her glorious curves without judgment. And damn, does she have them in all the right places. I need to calm down; these pants are getting a little uncomfortable. I continue to watch her as all shame I may have once had is completely out the window now. I am still staring at her ass when she turns around. I slowly make my way up her body, just trying to memorize everything I possibly can for myself for later. I start going up as she is an off-the-shoulder crop top that enhances her breast in the most delectable way. I stare at her perfect tits for a moment more before I continue up to finally see her face. When I get to her face, not only is she the most beautiful womanI have ever seen, but she is staring right back at me as if she knew I was looking at her. Unsurprised by the fact that the woman I was staring at was my mystery woman that I had invited here tonight. What does surprise me is the hint of fear that I can barely make out on her face. I noticed her friend from work beside her, and it makes me wonder if the fear I saw was her fearing me or fearing that she got caught blowing me off.

Layla

FUCK! Fuck. Fuckity fuck!! I cannot seem to stop saying it as I down the entire drink in my hand and turn back to the bar for another one. I swore I was only going to have a couple of drinks tonight, but that does not seem to be what is happening now! Leah looks over at me like I have just lost my mind. Which is completely fair because I am starting to feel like that myself. "Girl, slow down, or we aren't going to be here long enough for me to find someone to fuck!" Leah shouts at me over the music. I am now pissed off because she had said she wanted to have a girl's night with me. Turns out that is not the case; she just wants to get laid and does not want to come out by herself. "I thought we were just here to have a good time. I did not realize you just convinced me to come out tonight just so that you could get laid by some random guy." I snapped at her. I really should not have snapped at her; my mood is not completely her fault. Though I feel like she lied to me, she could have just told me what she wanted to come out for and not told me that she wanted to hang out when she clearly did not. Leah just rolls her eyes at me like she has the right to be upset with me, tells me she is going to dance, and walks off to the dance floor. I am conflicted about what to do, and I can still feel my mystery man staring at me. So, I down the rest of my second drink and head to the dance floor. Once on the dance floor, I

find Leah grinding on two different guys. She just glances at me and winks like everything at the bar did not just happen. I just started dancing, trying to forget this night and all the bullshit around me. I have been dancing for a while, and I lost count of how many drinks I *have had, which I am going to regret heavily tomorrow, but for now, I cannot feel you know who's stare anymore, and I have completely forgotten why I am mad at Leah. The next song starts playing when I feel someone grab my arm. I turn to find Leah there; she has a huge smile and tells me she is heading out. She points to the tall blonde guy standing behind her with his hand way too close to her downstairs while standing in this crowd of people. I instantly remember why I was upset with her, but before I could comprehend what was happening and spit my drunken words out, she was practically running off the dance floor. Anger flares inside me, and I turn to try to get back into my good mood and start dancing again. However, when I turned back around, I came face to face with none other than my mystery man. He always captivates me and renders me speechless; we stand staring at each other for a moment before I finally get the courage to say something. When I open my mouth to speak to him though, the only thing that comes out instead is vomit. I have now puked all over the dance floor and, well my mystery man, considering he was directly in front of me. Lovely, this night is going absolutely nothing like I had hoped. My best friend left me drunk in the club alone, and I puked all over the gorgeous man I have ever seen. Just freaking great! I look at him, about to apologize, when I realize I am swaying. Silently begging myself not to pass out, my eyes start to close on their own, and I lose all control of my body. The only thing I can think about is hoping when I hit the floor, I do not fall into the vomit I just put there. But instead of the impact of the floor, I feel like I am floating and have that same odd sensation that I cannot place, only this time, it is running through my arms. This is the last memory I have before I completely pass out and fall into darkness.*

Step Into Darkness

Cameron

I continued to watch my mystery girl as she danced and seemed to be having a good time. I liked to watch her; I did not like all the random men that she was dancing with, which was an odd feeling for me. I should not feel possessive over a woman I do not know. Though she did not seem interested in any of them, she was just dancing, so that eased my possessiveness a lit bit. I did notice that she was downing drinks fast, and that had me a bit worried about her partying habits. Is this normal behavior for her, or did something happen that made her feel like she needed to forget? I am still seated in my booth, watching her dance, when her friend from earlier approaches her. She said something to my mystery girl and pointed to the tall blonde guy behind her, whom I can see from here is being really handsy even for a club. Before my girl can say anything, her friend takes off toward the exit with her; what I am going to guess is her good time for tonight.

Now irritated with her friend, I head down to the dance floor because I cannot believe that her friend just left her here drunk and alone. When I reach her, she turns, and we are now face to face again, and I swear I stop breathing. Being this close to her, looking so incredible, all I want to do is ravish her. I am getting hard again, so I take a few deep breaths and internally scold myself. I am still at a complete loss for words when she looks like she is about to say something. Instead of words, she pukes all over me and the dance floor. I am completely disgusted, but when I look up to say something, I see her eyes glazing over, and she starts to sway. She starts to fall, and without a second thought, I catch her and pick her up, bridle-

style, carrying her out of the club. As I am walking towards the front of the club with her in my arms, I realize that where our arms are touching, skin to skin, I feel that weird tingling sensation again. It seems much stronger when I am touching her verses while being watched by her. All I can think about as I am walking out is how odd this is but how satisfying it feels.

Chapter 4

CAMERON

I have no idea who this woman is. I do know that I need to know her, and I know that I am covered in her vomit, so that is lovely. I laid her on the backseat of my car as I drove to my house. Feeling like I had just kidnapped a lady, I tried reasoning with myself on why taking her with me was my only logical option. Passed out and drunk, anyone at that club could have taken advantage of her, and I would never allow someone else other than me to touch her. That came out more possessive than intended. Okay, but besides that, I have no idea her name or where she lives, so I could not take her home. She did not have her purse or wallet with her when all this occurred, so I have no information about her. Also, I am covered and puke, and I need to get cleaned up. I can do that while I wait for her to wake up. My house keeps are gone for the weekend, so no one will be at the house to be judgmental or make her feel uncomfortable. We make it to my place, and I carry her up to my room and lay her down on my bed. As much decency as I have, I did check her to see if she had a phone on her

but again, no such luck. I got to my bathroom, stripped down, and got in the shower to clean up. I am battling with myself over the events of this evening as I stew in the shower. How completely wreckless of her to not have anything on her. Something terrible could have happened, and she would not have been able to contact anyone for help! This shower was supposed to help calm me, but I am just all riled up instead.

I hear a faint knock on the bathroom door, and I freeze for a moment, waiting. I did not hear anything else, so I quickly turned the water off and reached for my towel, which was right outside the shower. I quickly dry the lower half of my body and throw on a pair of sweats so I am at least decent when I go back into the room. When I open the door from the bathroom, I see her, she is sitting on my bed crying. Seeing her crying, I lose all common sense and self-control; I run to the side of the bed and kneel beside her, trying to figure out what is wrong and why she is crying. When her tear-soaked face finally looks up at me, I am sure my heart breaks at the raw emotion in her eyes. I finally managed to speak to her for the first time, and all I could do was reassure her that everything was fine and that she was safe here. She looks at me intently and takes a few deep breaths to calm herself enough to speak. Then, she asks me where she is and what happened to her friend Leah. I explained to her that her friend had left with a tall blonde guy. I am almost positive that rage fills her features. I told her that I came over to see if she needed a ride home due to the amount of alcohol she consumed, and then she threw up all over me and the dance floor. At this point, I do not think her face could get any more red. I tried to assure her that it was okay and that she passed out after that. I told her I did not know where to find her belongings, and since I did not know who she was or where she lived, I brought her back to my place so that I could get cleaned up while I waited for her to wake up.

When I finally finished with the events of the night to bring us up to the present, she just sat there contemplating everything I had told her. Then she looked me dead in the eyes and said, "Why did you want me to meet you at the club at 9 pm?" As happy as I am that she has *her memory mostly intact, I cannot help the stab of pain I feel at the fact that she just confirmed that she blew me off on purpose. I just stare at her now with conflicting emotions. She clearly notices my turmoil; she chuckles to herself, "I do not know you. I do not even know your name. You asked me to meet you at the club to talk, and I did not know how to feel about that because I had no context as to what it was you wanted from me. Again, I do not know you and my friend Leah, and I already had plans to be at the club tonight before you ever gave me that note." I look down, staring at nothing but the floor. I find myself feeling foolish; of course I cannot blame her for that. I was literally in the shower, angry with her for how reckless she was tonight for not having her phone on her. I look back up, meeting her gaze head-on, "I am sorry, you are right. I should not be upset about you being cautious of someone you do not know. So, let me fix that. I am Cameron Magnolia." I reach my hand out to her, expecting her to shake it and tell me her name. Instead, she busts out laughing. I am completely dumbstruck; I have never had someone laugh in my face before, so I am unsure what to do.*

LAYLA

Did he just try to claim to be the one and only Cameron Magnolia? Did he think that was going to work? I mean, I know that I saw this guy at my work doing the walk, , through. Cameron Magnolia would never step low enough to show his face in our factory. I am running all of this through my head hysterically, laughing so hard I am certain I am crying. He is sitting in silence as I laugh. Once I calmed down enough, I looked over to him, expecting to see the look of guilt and defeat on his face from thinking that would work on me. But instead, when I look at him, I see confusion and, I think, hurt. Which now has me confused. Okay, say he really is Cameron; there is no way he would go out of his way this many times just to talk to me.

"Okay, say I believe you, which is a long shot just so we are both on the same page. Why would you come do the walk-through of such a small, pointless factory like ours? It clearly serves no bearing on the all-around money-making projects I am sure you work with on a day-to-day basis. Not to mention going out of your way to talk to me, let alone save me. I am not a wealthy person; I am no one of importance." I asked him. He looked frustrated and took a deep breath, saying, "Is that what people think of me? That I am just a wealthy snob who cares only about myself and other wealthy people?" I am even more puzzled now. He looks at the ground, then rocks back on his heels and up to his feet. He is now standing in front of me, and I had not realized this whole time that he was only in sweatpants. And boy, was my lower region not prepared for the sight before me, as a shiver ran all the way down my body and straight to my core. This overwhelming feeling of wanting to touch all his chiseled muscles takes over me. I cannot take my eyes off him and the tattoos that run all over his body. I am not in my right mind when I hear him clear his throat, and it snaps me back to reality. Once back, I realized that not only was I ogling him, but I had in fact, reached out and was running my hand down the outline of his abs. I am literally mortified all over again. I cannot bring myself to look at him after that. I feel a tingling sensation on my chin; realization dawns on me, and my eyes go wide as he brings my face to look at him. The tingles are coming from where his fingers are touching my skin. How odd.

When he removed his hand, I reached up to touch my chin where he was. I look at him, and he is looking at his hand the same way I feel. Did he feel that too? I glance back up to see him already watching me. "If you don't believe my words darlin, I will prove to you who I am."

And with that, he holds out his hand for me to take. Hesitantly, I took his hand. Those tingles are back, and I try to ignore them as he helps me to my feet. As I stand, I drop his hand and look around. I have been so distracted this whole time that I

have not even been paying attention to my own surroundings. The room we are in is dark, the walls a navy blue with off-white accents thrown in here and there. Off to the side of the room is what looks like a small sitting area with a couch and TV with some small end tables. I can feel his eyes on me while I take in the room around me. As I can now deduce it to be his bedroom, I turn back to him as he leads us out into a hallway. Walking down this hallway is like a time portal of his life with his family. There are several pictures hung all over the walls. They all look so happy, and that hurts my heart now, realizing how wrong I was and how much it probably hurts to look at all those memories you cannot make with them anymore. I feel like such a jerk for laughing at him, and I am quite sure I am red again

from embarrassment. If he sees it, he does not comment on it, though which I am currently grateful for at this moment.

We come to the end of the hall and down a set of beautiful marble stairs. Once we reach the bottom, he says, "I am sorry if I have caused you any kind of inconvenience. It is about 3 in the morning, and with the amount of alcohol you consumed tonight and then throwing up, I thought maybe some water or coffee and something to eat might help." I just nod because, at this point, I am completely shocked and way out of my element. I watch as he makes me some coffee, gives me a cup of water just in case, and makes me a sandwich. He lightly guided me to the kitchen island and motioned for me to have a seat. I started to eat the sandwich he made me when I finally came back to my senses. "You never answered my question earlier about why you wanted to meet with me to talk." I question him. He looks at me and swears I catch a glimpse of mischief in his eyes before he says, "I will answer your question darlin, if you tell me your name. You know mine now and have the proof to go with it, but I still do not know who you are." Oh my gosh! He is right. I am sure if I looked even more of an idiot right now, I would face-palm myself. "Layla, my name is Layla Nichols. I am so sorry. I did not even realize I had not introduced myself." And now I am rambling because I am in the presence of the one and only Cameron Magnolia! "Wait, your Cameron Magnolia, I cannot be here. I cannot be at your house right now. Oh, I am such an idiot; I am for sure losing my job this time. I must leave!" I am panicking and stuttering, feeling like I might pass out again.

Chapter 5

CAMERON

~

"Layla darlin, try to calm down, breathe slow deep breaths. It is going to be okay. Please calm down! I did not mean to upset you." I try to reassure her that everything is going to be okay. But she looks like she is going to pass out again. A few moments later, and surely enough, she loses consciousness again. I catch her quickly before she smacks her head on the counter. Honestly, at this point, I have no idea what just happened, and with the craziness of tonight, I am exhausted. I pick Layla up bridal style and carry her back upstairs to my room. I thought about putting her in the guest room, but I prefer to have her near me. I need to keep an eye on her and make sure she is okay. At least, that is what I keep trying to convince myself is the reason. I lay her back down in my bed and covered her up. I crack the bathroom door with the light on in case she wakes up and needs to use it. I grab an extra blanket from my closet and lie down on the couch across the room. My bed is plenty big enough, but I am not trying to scare her; she already seems pretty shaken up.

I lay on the couch positioned so I could see her asleep on my bed. I wish I knew what it was about this girl that drew me in so much. I keep trying to tell myself that I brought her here to get cleaned up and wait for her to wake up. But truth be told, I have never brought a woman to my house before. It was never a line I wanted to cross. Bringing women to my house makes the moment with them seem more personal than it ever was. But with Layla, I never even hesitated. Earlier, when I stood to prove to her who I was, it was almost like she was in a trance. Like she was free from whatever held her back, the way she looked at me was intoxicating. Then, without even thinking, she just reached out and touched me. She started tracing the lines of my chest tattoos all the way down till she reached my abs. I was breathing heavily and willing myself not to get hard right there in front of her. I internally groaned as I remembered what it felt like to have her fingertips tracing my toned stomach; the tingling was almost unbearable as she traced lower and lower on my abdomen. There was no hiding how much I wanted her at that moment, but she did not seem to be fully aware of what she was doing. As much as I wanted to let her keep exploring, I needed to stop her. I cleared my throat, and it was like whatever was holding her captive snapped and brought her back to reality. She looked at me and then at her hand that was still on my lower abdomen. Her eyes went wide, and she pulled her hand away like I burned her. The poor girl's face was so red, like a tomato, and she would not look at me. Good god, that is only turning me on more; remember how adorable she looked while embarrassed? At this rate, I am never going to be able to fall asleep. Needing the relief so I can get some sleep, I pull my dick out of my sweatpants and start stroking as I watch Layla sleep in my bed. Wishing so badly that I could be up there with her. Touching her soft skin and feeling those amazing tingles we feel when we touch. I stroke faster, remembering her in the club, grinding and shaking her ass in those amazingly tight jeans. "Oh god." I say out loud as I cum hard, remembering how she had traced my muscles so tenderly earlier. I only feel slightly better as I realize I have made a huge mess and now need to go clean up again and grab a new blanket. After letting out some more pent-up tension in the shower a couple more times, I climb out feeling lighter, like I can sleep now. I put on clean sweatpants, *grabbed a new blanket, and climbed back onto the couch to try to get some kind of sleep before Layla woke up.*

Layla

I start to stir, not even remembering when I fell asleep. I roll over only to realize I'm in bed; I do not remember getting home or how I got to bed. I really must have had too much to drink; that is the last time I go out with Leah I swear. I slowly open my eyes and rub my hands over them. I throw my feet over the side and open my eyes. The problem is, that I did not seem to make it home, and this is not my bed. I glance around the room, and all the memories from last night come flooding back. I jump up and run to the bathroom and throw up. I sit back on my heels and look around the lavish bathroom. It's gorgeous with its giant stand-up shower that could easily fit three of me, and on the other side of the room is an enormous stand-alone bathtub! Talk about bathroom goals! I got up and rinsed my face off, walking back out into the bedroom, I noticed I was the only one in the bed. Which I

am grateful for, but I also have a sense of sadness. How odd. As I am walking to the door that I am almost positive has a hallway on the other side. I glance over, and there he is; Cameron is asleep on the couch in his sitting area.

I swear I am dreaming. I walk over to where he is sleeping awkwardly spread on the couch. I know that he cannot be comfortable, yet he chooses to sleep on the couch rather then in bed beside me. I seem to be really upset about that. I feel overly conflicted about it. As I stride closer to him, his features become more noticeable in the dark room. He looks so relaxed and peaceful. I noticed the blanket he was using had made its way to the floor. So, I can see his entire upper body on display. What I see, however, is a drool-worthy masterpiece of muscles and artwork. Starting at his face I take in his sharp jawline with a light dusting of a beard trying to show. I work my way down as I take in every bit of him. I do not think I have ever wanted someone so bad in my life. He is gorgeous. I follow his tanned skin all the way down to the detailed V that cuts into the top of his low-hanging sweats. I can see every vein trying to make its appearance on his arms, and every slow breath he takes as he sleeps is almost calming as I watch him. I finally pulled myself out of my thoughts and reached down to pick up his blanket that had fallen to the floor. As I do so, my arm slightly grazes his. I instantly feel the tingles and pray to the heavens that I did not wake him. I pause for a moment and wait. I do not hear anything, so I continue to bend over and pick up the blanket. As I stand back up, I glance over, only to notice the impressively large tent in his sweats. I whip around to find him already watching me. "Good morning, Layla." He stated casually like his monster of a penis was not just in my face as I stood back up. "Have you been awake long?" he asks, noticing my hesitancy. "Long enough to remember what happened last night, which was also long enough for me to run to your extravagant bathroom to throw up again." I state, trying to keep the quiver out of my voice. He catches it anyway and sits up right away, pulling me to sit next to him on the couch. I know that I do not know him and really should not be allowing him to touch me, let alone pull me into his side for comfort. But he makes me feel so comfortable that I do not even try to fight him. I mean, I am an emotional wreck right now, though, so my fight or flight mode could just be all jacked up.

He lifts my chin so I am looking at him. His eyes show so much concern for me that I find myself just melting into the warmth of his body for comfort. He does not hesitate to wrap me into his side even more as I begin to sob into him. "I thought she was my best friend.

How could she leave me there like that! It is girl code number one; you never leave the other drunk and unattended!" I feel like I am shouting, and he just hums and runs his fingers through my hair as if he is trying to comfort me in any way he can. After a while of crying, I finally calmed down and looked up at him. He is already looking at me, and I just wait for the insults about how dramatic I am being for nothing. But instead, he stands and picks me up bridal style, which seems to be his favorite way to carry me. He walks us to the bathroom, and I start to panic, but he gently sets me down on the bathroom counter. "You have no reason to fear me. I understand that you do not know me, and I promise I will fix that, but know that I will never hurt you. Now that you seem calmer, I am going to draw you a bath to help you relax and feel better. Take as long as you want. I will get some of my sweats and put them on the bed for you to wear while I wash your clothes. Once you are dressed and ready, I will be downstairs." He starts the water in the huge bathtub and starts putting in different oils and salts. He gives me a shy smile, points to a towel hanging on the wall, and walks out of the bathroom, closing the door behind him.

I am pretty sure every part of my insides just melted. I have not had great relationships in the past. Most of the guys I dated just wanted to get into my pants. This generation truly sucks when it comes to moral values. Anywho, when I would not sleep with them, theywould start the insults. How I was just a big tease and that after making them wait a couple weeks or even a month for the ones that were dedicated to getting what they wanted. That I owed them for the trouble they went through with me. It would gut me every time; I just wanted that romantic love. Someone who saw me for me and not just what I could give them. I want someone who is going to love me and cherish me the way I would them. Not a guy who pretends, a man who is real. I gave up on men about six months ago when the last guy I dated did not understand what the word No meant. As much as the constant rejection and mean words hurt. I can take that from the others. But Roman was my last straw with men. We had been seeing each other for about a month, and I really liked him. We seemed to have several things in common, from our favorite foods to the kinds of movies and TV shows we were into. One night, he was over at my place, and we were watching the first Jurassic World movie. I had a long 12-hour shift that day, and I had apparently fallen asleep during the movie. Roman knew that I was not ready to sleep with him yet. He knew that I was waiting for someone permanent in my life. But I was awakened by him fondling my breasts. Which was not a super huge deal until I opened my eyes to realize that he was completely naked on top of me and had removed my shorts while I was sleeping. I started to panic and realized he had my arms pinned above me with one hand. I was stuck and could not get away. I tried to twist and push against him to get free, but I was losing hope quickly. I paused for a moment to catch my breath. "There you go, doll; just relax, and this will be quick." He smirked at me like he was not doing anything wrong. He still had my hands pinned and grabbed his cock in his other hand, starting to guide it towards my opening. I started to sob, and at a last attempt to get free, I brought my knee up and managed to catch him right in the balls. He instantly let go of me and doubled over. I quickly jumped up and ran to my bathroom, and locked myself in. As soon as I had the door locked, Roman was on the other side banging on it, yelling at me to come out, and how much of a bitch, I was for kneeing him. I told him we were over and to leave my apartment and never come back. I never wanted to see him again! "This is not over, Layla! You may have won this round, but I will be back, and I will have you." He threatened, and then all I heard was the front door slam shut. Absolutely terrified, I spent the rest of that night locked in my bathroom, a complete mess.

As I come back to reality, I realize that not only am I still in Cameron's bathtub, but I am also crying, and my water is cold. I am now wondering how long I was stuck in that nightmare of a memory. I take a deep breath to try to calm my racing heart and quickly wash up. I stepped out of the tub, dried myself with the towel he had motioned to, and headed out of the bathroom in search of the sweats he promised. I glance into the bedroom just to verify that Cameron is not in there before I walk out in only a towel. Luckily, he has kept his word and is nowhere to be found. I do, however, find the sweats he left me on the bed. He set out a pair of sweatpants and a large, long-sleeve shirt. I hurried and put them on. Realizing now how cold I was before I had the warmth of clothes that I am currently swimming in.

Chapter 6

CAMERON

~

As soon as I walk out of my bathroom, I stand in the bedroom listening. I have no idea what I am doing, and I am way over my head right now. I hear some splashing and assume Layla is in the bathtub. Knowing she took the offer and got in to relax some relaxes me. I hope she feels comfortable here, and I do not want her to feel pressured or uneasy at all. I make my way down to the kitchen and make Layla and I some scrambled eggs and bacon. I am unsure how long she will be, but at least there will be food to heat up when she comes down. I cannot keep my mind to myself as I eat my food. It keeps reaching her and everything that has happened. I feel terrible about her friend and the clear betrayal that Layla is feeling from her actions. I was also mad about last night. I finish my breakfast, rinse my plate, and put it into the dishwasher. Heading to the living room, I stop at the bottom of the stairs, contemplating if I should go check on her or not. I tiptoe to the bedroom door, like the major creeper I seem to have become in the last 24 hours. I do not hear anything, completely forgetting that my room is soundproof. So, I slowly opened my bedroom door and silently walked to the bathroom door. As I get closer, I hear sniffling and can only guess that she is crying again. But I did not want to barge in on her naked in the tub, so I sighed and walked back out and down to the living room. Knowing that there is nothing more I can do *for her at this moment, I flip on the TV for some kind of distraction while I wait for her.*

Mindlessly staring at the TV, I must have dozed off for a bit. I sit up in a panic when I feel the couch dip. I shake off my sleep and realize that Layla has finally descended from upstairs. I stare in awe at how beautiful she is in my clothes. I must have been staring too long because I heard her clear her throat, and when I looked up, she had the cutest blush on her face. "Sorry darlin, I've just never shared clothes with anyone, and you look way better in them than I do." I rasp out. Her eyes widened, and for a moment, I thought I may have said the wrong thing. "You have never shared clothes with someone before?" she asked, almost in amazement. "That is correct. I do not go out very often, therefore I do not really meet people unless they are on a work-related basis. To be honest, you are the first woman to ever even be in my house other than the cleaning staff." Her mouth falls open, and she is gaping at me like I have lost my mind. Then I see something cross her features, and I am unsure if I saw hurt or anger, maybe even both? "Why does that seem so outrageous to you?" I asked her. "You expect me to believe that besides your housekeepers, you have never had other women in this house?" She seems slightly bitter, and I think I catch a bit of jealousy from it. Hm, she doesn't seem to believe me. But I am also confused because why would I lie to her. "Layla, why would I lie to you?" I ask softly, not wanting her to feel as though she cannot trust me. "Because everyone lies. You are very wealthy and likely have women falling all over you. I have never met a guy who hasn't lied to me." She seems really upset, and honestly, I am not sure how to make her feel better or believe me. "I am sorry for the men who have mistreated you in the past, Layla. But I am not them, and I can assure you darlin I have no reason or intention of lying to you. I hope that you can trust me that I am telling you the truth." She stares off for a moment like she is deep in thought, *and I wish so deeply that I knew what was going on inside her head. After a while of us sitting in silence, she spoke, and the raw emotion in her voice took me by surprise. "I will do my best to trust you. But know that I have been wronged several times, and it is very hard." I reach for her, and she slowly slides over to rest against me. I take a moment to twirl her hair around my finger a couple of times before I remember that she hasn't eaten breakfast. "Are you hungry darlin ? I made scrambled eggs and bacon earlier. I can heat it back up for you if you would like." She nods, and I stand to reheat her food for her. When I came back to the living room, I found her cuddled up under the throw blanket that was hanging on the back of the couch. She sits up as I go around the couch, and I sit beside her and hand her the plate. Our fingers grazed as we transferred the plate, and I felt the tingles. "Layla, do you feel those too?" I asked her hesitantly. She just nods her head as she eats, though I see the slight pink crawling up to her cheeks. "Do you know what it is?" she asks as she swallows her bite of food. "No, I have never experienced anything like it before. But if I am being honest, I really enjoy how it feels." I stutter, blush, and feel like my face is on fire. We sit in silence the rest of the time she eats, and I hope I didn't make her feel weird by admitting that I like the tingles we share. When she finishes her food, we go to the kitchen to put her plate away and get something to drink. She turns to me, "I think they feel soothing. I have never had that before so I guess I enjoy them too. However, not to be rude, but do you plan on taking me home? I do need to find my purse and phone." I just grin at her and go to the laundry to get her clothes from the dryer. As I walk into the kitchen to give her her clothes, there is a knock at the door. I tell her where the downstairs bathroom is so she can change, and I head to the front door.*

LAYLA

I go into the downstairs bathroom to change back into my clothes. I am a little sad. I must take hisclothes off; they were so soft! However, since he washed my clothes, they now smell like him. As I walked out to the living room, I heard people talking. I had completely forgotten that someone had been at the door. I round the corner into the living room to find Cameron talking with two police officers. They all turn to look at me as I approach them; Cameron reaches for me and motions for me to have a seat. "Good morning, Miss Nichols. We have some items that we believe belong to you." The officer hands me my purse. Inside are my wallet, cell phone, and everything else I had left behind at the club last night. Besides my dignity, of course. "Thank you, officer; we were just going to head down to the club to try and find these." I

state. The two officers look at each other in confusion, which in turn makes me feel confused and slightly uneasy. "Miss Nichols, we have to ask you some questions about last night. See, we have had some interesting calls about you." Turning to look at Cameron, he gives me a small, reassuring smile. "Alright, well let's get to it, I guess." I whisper, trying not to show how uneasy I am right now. "So first of all, we got a call from the club last night stating that you were kidnapped. They have witnesses saying they saw Mr. Magnolia carry you out of the building and into his car. Which is how we were able to come across your items here." He motions to my purse on the table. I glance at Cameron, whose face is pretty red. I kind of chuckled seeing him look like that. "Miss, can you take us through last night's events."

One of the officers asks. "Yes, of course. Last night, I had plans to go out for a few drinks with my friend Leah; we met at the club around 9 pm. We got our drinks and headed to the dance floor. I am not a drinker and must have been feeling stressed because I lost track of how many drinks I had, had. My friend Leah bailed on me to get lucky, and Mr. Magnolia came over after seeing what my friend had done to see if I needed a ride home. However, I ended up throwing up all over him and the dance floor, then passed out." I am pretty sure my face is red now from how embarrassed I am about this whole situation. "That all lines up with what we were told for the most part, but how did you end up back here and not at home?" The officer questions. "Well, that's my fault, sir. After Layla passed out, I carried her to my car and intended to take her home, but as I started driving, I realized that I didn't know where she lived. So, I brought her back here so I could get cleaned up from the puke, and I planned on taking her home this morning once she was awake and lucid." he states. "When I woke up this morning, I was confused at first, but Cameron explained why I was here, and then after remembering my friend leaving me drunk and alone in the club last night, I kind of had an emotional breakdown. So, Cameron offered for me to take a bath and relax while he washed my puke-covered clothes for me. I just went to change so we could head back to find my belongings and go home." I assure them. "Well, ma'am the other call we got was from one of your neighbors. I am sorry to inform you, but your apartment was broken into last night." He states as lightly as he can. My eyes go wide and start to mist over, and before I know it, I am crying again. "I am very sorry, Miss Nichols. We can escort you home if you would like, and we can go through everything with you to see what is missing." I finally wipe my tears and look over at Cameron, who surprisingly isn't looking at me like normal. He is staring off and looks angry. "I appreciate all of your help, Cameron. But I don't want to burden you any more than I already have. I will let the officers escort me home." I say in a shaky voice. I stand to leave when he grabs my hand and says, "You are not a burden, Layla, and I will not have you going there alone. I will drive you, and the officers can either lead or follow." He states in a no-argument tone. I release the breath I didn't realize I was holding as he stands and places his hand on my lower back, leading me to his car.

We drive in silence to my apartment other than the directions I am giving Cameron. We pull into the parking lot and notice another set of police officers already there. I try to stay calm, but I feel so uneasy that I am starting to get lightheaded. "I don't think I can do this." I spew between deep breaths. Cameron reaches over and grabs my hand, "I am right here, Layla. Breathe with me, or you are going to black out again okay? Close your eyes and focus on the tingles and your breath." I do as he says and close my eyes. Everything around me is gone except for the tingling in my hands, where he is rubbing his thumbs along my palms. I take a nice deep breath, and as I inhale, all I smell is him. I focus on bringing that scent to life, and It's musky but with a hint of spice and vanilla. As I focus only on these things, I feel myself calming back to a normal state of mind. I open my eyes to meet his eyes. They are green, and I haven't stopped long enough to see them before. They are not super bright, but they remind me of the forest. They are different shades of green mixed together with specs of brown floating around. "You have the most beautiful eyes I have ever seen." As I hear my own voice, I come back to reality. Cameron sits there smiling and enjoying my embarrassment as my eyes are now wide with a hand over my mouth, not believing I just said that out loud.

Chapter 7

LAYLA

~

I swear I need to get a grip when I am around Cameron! I cannot believe I just said that! I scrambled out of his car to get some space from him. I am now thinking that whatever is waiting for me in my apartment is way less concerning than what just happened. As I walk up to the door of my apartment, I've got Cameron right on my heels and the officers not far behind him. I reach my door and find more police officers inside. They greeted me with an apologetic smile. I glance around to see nothing but complete chaos. My furniture is overturned, and all my knick-knacks have been broken. I pass the officers in shock as I walk all around my apartment to see that the whole space is in complete disarray. "As far as I can tell, nothing seems to be missing. Though everything is ruined." I tell the officers. My entire bed, sheets and blankets included, have been slashed through with some kind of large knife. Every picture in the whole place has been smashed. Dishes from the kitchen have been busted on the floor, and they plugged the kitchen sink and turned on the water. It was overflowing water all over for who knows how long until the police officers got here. As I am wandering around my bedroom, I catch a whiff of something potent. It gets stronger as I get closer to my dresser. I open the drawer slowly and instantly realize that the smell is gasoline. Every dresser drawer has been soaked in gas, ruining all my clothes. I was in such shock that I didn't realize I was crying until I felt tingles swipe across my face as Cameron wiped a tear from my cheek. As soon as I looked up and we made eye contact, I crumbled. Every bit of strength I had left to hold my mental state together is gone. I had worked so hard to get everything I had, and just like that, it's all gone. I sit on the floor with Cameron sitting in front of me. At this point, I am ugly, crying so hard I can't speak. I feel like I am hyperventilating. Cameron doesn't even try to talk to me, full-on, knowing I wouldn't be able to respond. He just sits here with me until I can calm down. "What am I supposed to do now?" I ask the officers who also haven't left yet. "Well, we have taken pictures and notes of everything; we will proceed with our investigation. Do you have any kind of renters insurance to help cover the damaged items?" the officer asks. "No, sir, I don't. I couldn't afford the extra when I moved in here and never thought to update it after getting settled." I say quietly. Feeling small in front of Cameron for the first time since I met him. I look down, feeling ashamed that I am not only in such a lower social class than him but I now have nothing to my name after working so hard to get here. Without looking up, I tell everyone thank you and that it is fine for them to leave. I turn my back on them and start to get busy cleaning up the mess I call my home. I hear footsteps, and after a few hushed conversations in the other room, the front door opens and then closes, signaling that they have gone. As soon as the front door closes, I burst into tears all over again.

CAMERON

I am completely speechless. I have never seen so much chaos. All of Layla's belongings are ruined, absolutely everything.. From her furnishings to her cookware, her bedding, and even every item of her clothing. I have no idea how she must be feeling right now, but it obviously isn't good. This wasn't a normal break-in; this was intentional and violent. I feel my pulse quicken just thinking about what could have happened if she had been home last night. I wipe away one of her tears, and when she meets my eyes, her entire resolve breaks. I sit with her on the floor for a long while as she gets it all out. There is nothing I can say to make any of this better, so I just decided to sit with her just to be here for her. Once she is calmer, she talks with the officer a bit. It hit me hard to hear her say that she didn't have renters' insurance because she couldn't afford it. After that, I noticed a shift in her. She dropped her head, and shame filled her features. The refusal to look at me just gutted me to the core. She feels less than me, and I won't stand for that. "Thank you for all your help; you can all go." She says without looking up, then turns her back to us. I can see the pity in the officer's eyes that there isn't anything more they can do for her. We all walk to the living room; they share hushed conversations about leaving an officer outside in case the person comes back. I told the officers that I was going to stay with her. No way in hell was I going to let her stay here by herself. They nod to me and leave. As soon as the door closed, I heard her burst into tears again. Pain rips through me at what she is having to deal with. I don't want to be in her space, so I start picking up the pieces of plate that are smashed all over the kitchen floor.

After a bit, I don't hear her crying anymore. So, I went out of the kitchen and into her bedroom, there, I found her asleep on the floor. Her couch isn't as sliced up as her bed, so I flip it upright and carry her to the couch. I find an untouched blanket in the top of a closet and cover her up. I stare at her, just taking her in. Layla is a disheveled mess, but damn if she isn't still the most beautiful woman I have ever seen. I peel myself away and start cleaning up the mess around us. I looked at my watch and realized it was 1 am. There is nowhere to sleep since her bed is ruined and her floors are hardwood. So, hoping for the best, I climb onto the couch beside Layla, trying not to wake her. I managed to get under the blanket, and she turned over, startled, and shoved me off the couch. "Ouch" I say after hitting the floor with a heavy thud. "Cameron?" Layla asks, surprised. "Yeah, darlin it's me." I rasp out from the floor. "Oh my gosh Cameron, I'm so sorry I thought...Wait, what are you doing here?" She says, cutting off her previous statement. "Darling, I never left. I am not going to leave you here by yourself after what has happened here." I told her. Her eyes widened, realizing I was here when she cried herself to sleep. Sitting up, she looks around at everything I have cleaned up while she slept. "You didn't have to clean any of this. It's not your problem or your fault; it happened; its mine, and I will handle it." She speaks. Now, confirming what I suspected. She knows who did this to her apartment and why. "Why are you protecting the person who did this to you? You could have told the cops when they were here, and then maybe I wouldn't have been shoved off the couch." I say, trying to lighten the air around us. She turns to me with eyes wider now, like she didn't think I would make the connection that she knew who it was. "You don't understand. It's not that simple. I thought that he let it go and moved on; I haven't heard from him in 6 months." She looks so fragile and broken as she speaks. "I can tell that you don't want to talk about darlin. But for me to help you, I need to know what happened and who he is." I say slowly as I pick her up and sit back down on the couch with her in my lap. She shook her head like she was trying to shake away the memory. This causes her entire body to start shaking. I wrap the blanket around her and hug her to me. "I can't." She stumbles on her words. "Layla, I've got you! I promise darlin, I am not going to let anything bad happen to you. But I need you to talk to me, okay?" I try to plead softly. She nods and takes a deep breath. "His name is Roman. I started seeing him 7 months ago., I wasn't ready to sleep with him, and I thought that he understood that. We had been seeing each other for a month. One night he was over here, we were watching a movie, and I had fallen asleep. I had worked 12 hours that day and was up early. He had taken my shorts off while I was asleep. He was getting ready to enter me when I woke up. I awoke to him fondling my breasts, and when I was awake enough to realize what was happening, I freaked out. I was panicking and trying to get away from him, but he had me pinned to the couch, and I could barely move. I could feel him at my entrance, getting ready to push into me. As a last effort to get free, I brought my knee up and luckily made contact. He let go of my hands, and I ran to the bathroom, locking myself in. He was threatening me through the door. Telling me that this wasn't over and that he would have me no matter what. After that, he finally left. I haven't heard from him since. I spent the rest of that night locked in my bathroom, terrified to leave." She sobbed. I am beyond pissed; just trying to keep it together for her. "Why didn't you call the cops?" I asked quietly. "I was scared and humiliated. I have been called so many terrible things by guys because I wouldn't sleep with them. And I was afraid of someone else telling me I was just a tease and had it coming." She looks full of shame, and I am doing my best to keep my anger in check. How could people make her feel like this about herself? "Darling, you are not a tease, nor did you deserve to be treated that way. Hell, I have wanted to do some obscene things with you on a constant basis since I met you! But none of that is something you have gone out of your way to make me feel. Nor is it my right to just take from you what I want without your consent." I admit. Her face is so red I'm pretty sure she would make a tomato jealous. "Tell me something beautiful. Have you ever slept with anyone?" I question her. I am almost positive the answer is no. "I, no, I haven't." she stutters out. The satisfaction I feel in my chest is overwhelming. "Why is that?" I pry. "I'm not sure to be honest. All the guys I've ever dated, they always demanded it. But to me, it's something that should be earned and cherished. So, I guess I have been waiting for someone to share it with. Someone who would cherish me and what we could be together. Not someone who is going to demand it, as if it was their right to have it just for buying me dinner." She kind of chuckles at the end, though I can't help but admire her strength. "I love that." I whispered in her ear. "Darlin, you know I can't let you stay here, right?" Hoping she understands. "But this is my home. I have worked so hard to get here!" She is trying not to break down again, so I give her a small squeeze. "I don't know where you started. But I am proud of you for getting here on your own. However, you are not alone anymore, and I will not let you be in harm's way staying here." I state firmly. "Where am I going to go, Cameron? This was the only place in my budget. I can't afford to get a new place, especially not now." She argues. I smile at her, and her eyes widen. "No, Cameron, you have already done so much for me." She tries to plead. "Layla, I insist you stay with me. It's just me at the house, and I have a guest room you can stay in." I try to say smoothly because I am freaking out on the inside! "That won't work, isn't it a conflict of interest because of my work? I will likely lose my job if I haven't already because of what happened on Friday." She seems so frustrated now. "Speaking of Friday what happened exactly?" I asked her curiously since we haven't had the time to discuss it as I had planned. "I'm not sure. I remember looking through the window to the conference room, and something about you just seemed to draw me in. I had such a weird sensation course through me. I was trying to place it, and that must have been when everyone caught me staring." She is blushing something fierce now, and I feel that twitch in my pants at the thought of seeing her covered in the deep red blush from other activities. Shaking that thought away for now. "I felt it also, It's what made me look over at you." I admit. Reaching down, I grab her hand and whisper, "Just like the ones when we touch." Layla gives me a small smile. "Alright Cameron, I'll stay with you, but ONLY until I can find somewhere else to live. But what am I supposed to do about work?" She questions, uneasiness creeping into her features. "Well, you go back to work on Tuesday to verify you still have your job. Though I'm pretty sure no matter what, you will not be without one." I say determine.

LAYLA

I am in complete shock that I agreed to stay with Cameron until I can find a new place to live. That is so unlike me, especially since I just met this guy Friday night. I am also really excited, which I am trying to overpower with common sense. I have such a strong pull to this guy I barely know, and now I have just agreed to live with him. "Cameron, what about all my stuff? All my clothes and belongings are ruined." I am starting to panic now. "Breath darlin, I will take you shopping, and we can get you anything that you need. It's not a big deal." He states nonchalantly. "You don't have to do that; I have some money saved up. I guess I will just use that." I stammer. Before he can say anything else, I turn on my heels in search of any untouched items I can pack. Luckily, most of my hygiene products were not on the list of things to destroy, so I didn't have to buy new ones. Cameron is just standing near the kitchen counter, watching me as I bounce from here to there, gathering what I can. Once packed, we headed back down to his car and back to his house to unload what I had before we went shopping. As we pulled up to his house, there was another car there. I look over to gauge Cameron's reaction to the car in hopes of giving me some kind of hint on whether this is a good or bad thing. He seems confused for a moment, but it is replaced with indifference almost instantly. He parks beside the other car and slides out, making quick work of reaching my door and opening it for me. What a gentleman. He grabs my bags from the back, leaving me feeling useless as we walk to the house. Climbing the front steps, the front door swings open, and a lady in her mid-forties walks out, looking completely distraught. Not being able to see me past Cameron, she begins badgering him. "Cameron! Where have you been? I got here yesterday, and you were nowhere to be found! Are you trying to kill your mother? I have been calling you!" Cameron stops in his tracks, dropping my bags and grabbing his phone from his pocket. "I am so sorry Mother; it has been a busy and eventful last couple of days. I must have forgotten to check my phone." He apologizes. "What on earth could have you so preoccupied that you don't check your phone? It is usually glued to your hand." She asks completely flabbergasted at this point. Cameron picks my bags up and steps to the side. I am now standing directly in front of his mother. "Good Lord. Now, how can I blame you; this young lady is stunning!" She says, looking between Cameron and me. I am likely giving a tomato a run for its money right now, but I will try to pull it together. "It is nice to meet you, Mrs. Magnolia. I am Layla Nichols." I say with a smile. I reach out my hand to shake hers, hoping it isn't as sweaty as I think it is. She takes it instantly and folds it between hers, pulling me in for a hug instead. I look over to Cameron, pleading with my eyes for help. Instead, he grins wider and just shakes his head at me. Feeling defeated, I just let the woman hug me. It was such a warm embrace that I guess I didn't realize I needed it. Because when she finally pulls away, she has a look of concern on her face. That's when I feel tingles slide across my face, and I look up at Cameron, who is wiping tears from my face. He gives me a small smile. "Layla, are you okay, dear? I didn't mean to upset you!" Mrs. Magnolia rushes out. "No, it's not you. It's been a rough few days for me, and I guess I

didn't realize how much I just needed a motherly hug." I speak.

Chapter 8

LAYLA

~

As I stand there in the doorway, trying to pull myself together. Mrs. Magnolia just gives me a small smile while I compose myself. Cameron nods to his mom as she is standing in front of the doorway, letting her know we can go inside now. She looks confused at first, then realizes what he is saying and blushes a bit before sauntering into the house. I glance up at Cameron and see him smiling down at me, giving me the okay to continue into his home. We walked in, and Cameron took me in. Cameron took me up to the guestroom only to find his mother's stuff in there. He pauses at the door and turns to look at me with an apologetic smile. Calling down to his mother, who is still on the first floor, he asks her how long she will be staying with him. She responds, saying only a couple of days. "I know it isn't ideal, but you can have my bed if you would like until she leaves. I can sleep on the couch either in the sitting area or downstairs, however you are comfortable." Cameron states. I smile and respond without even thinking, "That is fine, but your bed is plenty big. I don't expect you to sleep on the couch." I speak. Cameron looks as shocked as I feel, and I'm the one who said it. "Are you sure darlin I don't want you to be uncomfortable at all. You will be staying here, and I want you to feel at home." Cameron states honestly. And for some reason, I feel something inside me click into place. As I stand there thinking about what he said, I decide that even though I am unsure why, I trust

Cameron. "It's okay Cameron, I trust you. And I believe that we can share a bed for a couple of nights and be okay." I reassure him. He looks relieved at the fact that I admitted I trusted him. He seemed like he was nervous that I didn't, But I mean, after everything he had done for me in the last couple of days, how could I not. I mean, he has admitted that he wants to do inappropriate things with me. Which should have concerned me, but he hasn't tried anything. Plus, let's be honest: I wanted to do some inappropriate things to him as well. Maybe sleeping in the same bed with him isn't the best idea. Thanks to my stupid mouth, I have already sealed that fate, though, so there is no going back now. Cameron Smiles at me like he just won the lottery and turns to walk down the hall to his room. Once in his room, he sets my stuff down in the sitting area. Telling me to go ahead and get cleaned up. Since we have been up so long, it's only about 10 am at this point. "I am going to grab a shower in the downstairs bathroom and make all of us some breakfast. Go ahead and come down when you're ready. After breakfast, we can head back into town and get some shopping done." Cameron states cheerfully. I smile at him shyly and nod my head. He walks around the room gathers himself some clean clothes, and heads out of the room.

CAMERON

I couldn't be happier to hear Layla say that she trusts me. I am elated that she not only agreed to stay in my room but said I could too. I was heading down to the main floor bathroom to get cleaned when my mom stopped me at the bottom of the stairs. "Cameron dear, care to explain what is happening with that gorgeous young lady?" my mom questions. She is grinning from ear to ear. My mom also knows that I don't bring women here. So, she knows something here is different. "It's kind of a long story, and most of it is her story to tell. She is getting cleaned up and will be down for breakfast after a bit. I'm going to get cleaned up in the bathroom down here and then start on Breakfast. If you want to know about her, just ask her. But she has been through a lot the last few days, so please don't push or pry for information." I speak. My mom, on the other hand, just smiles wider, and her eyes twinkle with mischief. "You like her." She states simply. Not even asking me the question she already knows the answer to. "Yes, very much." I say with a sigh. I step around my mother and head to the bathroom. After getting washed up, I start on breakfast. As to not being sure what all Layla likes, I just make a variety of foods. Pancakes, waffles, eggs, and I even put out some fresh fruit. Along with making coffee and getting out the orange juice and milk. As I was finishing setting the table with everything, my mom walked in to sit down. Eyes wide, she says, "well, you weren't kidding at all, were you." I just smiled at her. A few moments later, Layla walks in. Her eyes also go wide as she looks at the table. "Goodness Cameron, you don't cook like this all the time, do you? Because if I'm going to be staying here, I'm surely going to be putting on some weight." She laughs. I hadn't really told my mom what was going on, so I glanced at her after Layla had made the comment about staying here, and my mom looked completely flabbergasted. Layla notices my mom's expression before she can school it. "Sorry, Mrs. Magnolia, I guess we didn't really explain anything huh. This is probably such a shock. It was to me, to when Cameron suggested I stay here, and I didn't want to impose, but he wouldn't take no for an answer, so here we are." Layla said. "When did you two meet?" my mother asks. "Friday." I state casually. "Friday?" my mother asks again, confused. "Yes, I met Layla Friday while I was doing my tour at her work for the contract renewal." I stated. "I'm pretty sure I was going to be fired. I made such a complete fool of myself. I was walking up to lunch and just happened to glance over, and there he was in the conference room. I'm not sure what happened. The next thing I knew, my friend Leah *was nudging me, and I looked around to realize we had stopped, and I had been staring at him, and everyone else was now staring at me." Layla says her face is a bit red from confessing that to my mom. "I then wanted to know more about her and wrote her a note to meet me at Club Underground, So I could get to know her. However, she already had plans to go there with her friend Leah. So, the intern blew me off." I say, trying not to convey how upset I am about that. "To be fair, I didn't know him, not even his name. So, I didn't think it would be a wise decision to meet up with a stranger at a nightclub. But our night went completely downhill after all that." Layla says, trying to hold back from crying again. "Let's just say that Leah and I are not on good terms at this point in time, as she left me drunk and alone in the club so she could leave to get lucky with some stranger." Layla is wiping a tear away as my mother says, "That's girl code number 1! You never leave your friend drunk and alone. Ever!" Layla is just nodding her head. "So that's when I went down onto the dance floor to see if I could give her a ride home, but she ended up puking all over me and the dance floor. Then she passed out. I was going to take her home, but as I got in the car, I realized that I still didn't know her name either. She didn't have her purse or even a phone on her. So, I brought her here so I could get a shower and clean clothes." I continued. "I woke up as he was in the shower. At this point, I was panicking, waking up in some stranger's bed and having no recollection of what had happened. Once he came out, he explained what happened and why I was there. After finding out who he was and panicking about that, making me lose my job, I passed out again." Layla says, face-palming herself. My mother giggled at watching Layla rehash how she handled everything. "So, I carried her back upstairs and put her back in my bed, and I took the couch in my sitting area." I sighed. My mom seems to be enjoying this back-and-forth that we are doing with our recap of the last couple of days. "Yesterday morning, I woke up,* remembering everything that had happened. Cameron drew me a bath and washed my puke clothes for me. By the time we got done eating breakfast, my clothes were clean. As I went to change, the doorbell rang." She looks worried now. "I went and got the door as I sent her to get changed. You can relate to my surprise when I opened the door and found 2 cops standing on the other side." I spoke. "Cops! Good grief, son what did you do?" My mother questions. "Well, they were here for a couple of reasons. First, the people at the nightclub called in, telling the cops that Cameron kidnapped me. Which is kind of true. The second reason was that my neighbor had called in because my apartment had been broken into." Layla says. She laughed a bit after saying I kind of kidnapped her. However, it vanished as soon as she brought up her apartment. "Cameron, you tried to make kidnapping look romantic! Lucky for you, it seemed to work. But Layla, you were lucky to be here instead of at home." My mother said, whispering the last part. "You have no idea." Layla sighed. "So, I take it you just came back from your apartment when I stopped you guys at the front door. And that's why you're staying here for now?" Mother stated more than asked. "Yes. After we eat, we must go shopping. Because the person who broke into her apartment ruined all her stuff. Clothes, furniture, kitchenware, all of it. Luckily, right now, she only really needs clothes because I have everything else." Giving Layla a small smile. She returns it, but it doesn't reach her eyes. "Oh my! They really did that! Did they even steal anything or just break in to be a nuisance?" my mother asked sharply. "They were just trying to scare me. He thought that I had forgotten about him and felt safe again." Layla says quietly while staring at her food. "He?" My mother asked cautiously. "An ex-boyfriend. I won't scar you with the details, so let's just say he tried to take advantage of me, and when it didn't work in his favor, he threatened to have me no matter what. That was 6 months ago. And though I never forgot what happened, I *was starting to feel safe in my own place again. That is until yesterday." Layla says as she picks at her food. My mother looks at me with wide eyes, like she can't believe what she just heard. After a few moments and me nodding to let her know it was true, her face turned to pure horror at what had happened to Layla. "Layla had nowhere to go, and I was not letting her stay in that apartment anymore. I will not risk her safety, nor can I protect her if she isn't here." I saw my mom smile at me, and I could see pride fill her eyes. "Well, if you two don't mind, I would love to go shopping with you! I never had any girls, and helping you pick out some new clothes would really make my day!" My mom gives Layla an adoring smile, and I try not to laugh at how much she adores her already. "Of course! I would love that and could use another girl's opinion on some outfits." Layla states shyly.*

LAYLA

I was completely taken aback by Cameron's mother wanting to go shopping with us. But I wasn't against it. With the weird connection between Cameron and I, it would be nice to have a buffer. Also, I tell her I need another girl's opinion on some outfits, which is true. It will be nice to have a mother figure there. I know she isn't my mother, but she has been so kind to me, and honestly, my dad wasn't the biggest fan of me moving out here to go to college, and with my mom gone. I don't talk to my father at all. But when I was back home before my mom passed, she used to go shopping with me and help me pick out clothes. As we get ready to leave, Cameron suggests that we take his SUV since we may need the room for all the shopping bags. I try to assure him that I don't need that much stuff, but he just smiles, and his mother giggles. So, we ended up taking the SUV. I try to let Mrs.

Magnolia sits up front with her son, but she isn't having it and climbs in the back. Walking into the mall, I realize just how big it is and just how much of a mistake this is. I do not have the kind of money to shop here. I tried to explain on the car ride that we could just go to a thrift store, and I would get some stuff. But neither of them would even hear of it. They walked me to some well-known stores. And I picked out some clothes I like that are on sale. I see Cameron and his mother grabbing some items here and there, but they don't say anything, so I figure they are just shopping as well. After a few hours of shopping, Mrs. Magnolia coiled her arm through mine, and we walked off, leaving Cameron on a bench in the middle of an aisle. We walked around a corner, and I found that she had just dragged me to the lingerie store. My eyes went wide, and I looked over to find her grinning at me like the Cheshire cat. "This really isn't necessary! I can just stop at Walmart to grab some undergarments." I try to reason with her. "Oh honey, look at yourself! You are absolutely stunning, but that doesn't mean you can't make yourself nice, either. Plus, you are going to need something sexy to wear to bed while you're sharing a room with Cameron." Then she winks at me and waltzes into the store. I just stood there for a moment, dazed and bewildered by what she had just said. Because it sounds like she wants me to seduce her son. I let out a laugh that was way too loud, and I immediately heat up at my own outburst. But with not much choice, I walked in to find Mrs. Magnolia looking at matching underwear and bra sets. As awkward as I feel right now, I do need undergarments, so I go over and start to look at some as well. By the time we are finished, I have plenty of underwear and a couple of really inappropriate nightwear that Mrs. Magnolia insisted would look amazing on me. By this time, it's around 1 pm, so we stop at the food court and grab a late lunch. We had some easy conversations during lunch, nothing overbearing. After lunch, we headed back to Cameron's house, and I swear by the time we got inside I'm ready to collapse. I follow Cameron up the stairs and into his bedroom. He sets all of the shopping bags down in the lounge area of his room. Turning to me, he says, "While my mom is here, I will make space for your clothes in my closet for you." I am instantly blushing at the thought of our clothes intermingling. I try to shake it off, but he sees it before I get a handle on it and smiles widely at me. I whispered a thank you, and he moved to his closet to start making space for my belongings. As soon as he is in the large walk-in, I collapse on the couch, starting to go through all the new clothes I just got. I was about halfway through my second bag when he joined me on the couch. He grabs a bag to help me, and before I can do anything, he has reached in and pulled out some of the 'nightwear' his mom insisted I should get. I go to take it from him, but he moves away. Standing until he is on the other side of the small coffee table. Afraid of the judgment I might see in his face, I couldn't bring myself to look at him. I am mortified by the thought of him seeing these, especially after everything he knows about me. "Layla" he calls to me. But I couldn't figure out his voice, and I was confused. He sounds out of breath, and I don't know why. "Layla, look at me." He is stern but doesn't sound disgusted like I thought he would, so I break and slowly look up to meet his gaze. He is looking at me so intently I flush and look away. I am officially squirming under the heat I feel radiating off him in waves. "Layla, who is this lingerie for?" He sounds breathy and impatient now. "No one. I just thought it looked cute." I sputter in my own words, feeling the wave of embarrassment hit me full force. I am totally regretting his mother talking me into getting these dang nighties! So caught up in my own mental anguish, I didn't realize that Cameron had moved to kneel in front of me, so when I looked up from my lap, I jumped a bit. His heated gaze was so strong on me, that I flushed uncomfortably. "I've been doing my best to control my want for you since the day I met you. I swear, Layla just thinking of you wearing this sexy nighty for anyone other than me will break all resolve I've got left." My breath gone. Did I just forget how to breathe?

Good grief, Layla get it together. Wait, did he just say he wanted me to wear this for him? Damn, his mother and being right! "You want me to wear these for you?" I squeaked out. "Can I show you something?" He asks me. Gaze was still hot and locked onto mine. I feel like I am in a daze. I nod my head yes, almost on autopilot. He takes my hand in his and slowly moves it down his body until it rests on his very huge and hard cock. I gasp and instinctively try to pull away. He doesn't let me, though. He does nothing else other than keep my hand pressed against his pants over his hard-on. He waits until I calm down and comes back to his eyes. "Layla darling, yes. Yes, I do. You are stunning, and the pull I have to you is so strong and like nothing I have ever felt before, and if I had to sit here and know that you were wearing these for some other guy, I would probably go feral." He seems panicked, and I'm not. Which is odd with our current circumstances. He is sitting on the couch beside me now, rambling like an adorable idiot for spilling how he is feeling, and all I can think about after everything he just said to me is to mount him! So, true to my ludicrous brain, without a second thought, I swung my leg over his lap in a blur of motion and smashed my lips to his. He is frozen at first, completely ambushed by my sudden change of mood. After a moment, he gets his bearings though. His mouth moved on mine with perfect skill. Our constant connective tingles are in full force, and I am in sensory overload. "Fuck, Layla!" Cameron groans as he grabs ahold of my ass, pulling me as close to his body as he can in this position. I unconsciously Start to grind on his already throbbing cock beneath me. Every time it spasms, it hits my bud right in the perfect spot. I am moaning and not realizing that I am straight up riding him with clothes on. Cameron doesn't seem to care at all; as his lips leave mine, I hear his heavy breathing. I feel the tingles as he moves down my jaw to my neck. Heat fills me more as his breath and tongue glide down my neck to my collarbone. I let out a heavy groan when he nips the space where *my neck and collarbone come together. "Layla, Baby girl if you don't stop riding me like that I'm going to cum in my pants." Cameron all but whisper yells into my neck. His voice is straining like he is trying to hold back. "And that would be bad?" I moaned out. "Fuck darlin I would rather have it any other way with you then in my pants like a damn teenage boy!" He is full body shuddering. Anything he can do to not get off in his pants. "I'm not selfish Cameron." I pick up my pace till I'm full-on shuddering now. I moan out as I hit my release. I keep pumping slowly to keep up my aftershocks for as long as I can. "Did you get it baby girl?" He asks, his voice husky and on edge. "Yes, did you?" He sets his head back on the couch to look at the ceiling. I take that as a no due to his previous statement. I climbed off him, realizing for the first time that he had changed into sweats while he was in the walk-in. He still isn't looking at me. I slide between his legs once he feels me move his legs apart. His head whips down to look at me. "Pants off, sugar." I say in my most sultry tone I can work up. I've never done this, to be honest, but I will not let him go without when he sat there letting me take complete advantage of him for myself. His eyes widened, and I started to feel selfconscious. But I mask it and raise my eyebrow questioningly. He must get that I'm serious and rushes to take them off. Once they are off I get a first look at the monster he has been hiding in there and that I just used to please myself. Now I think it's my eyes that were wide because when I look back at Cameron, he has a cocky smirk on his face. I school my features quickly, and I reach out and grip it. It's so big I can't get my fingers all the way around, and I would need another half a hand to cover the whole thing length-wise. I gulp and meet his eyes. "Layla darlin, you don't have to don't have to do this. I can take care of it." With a little chuckle, he continues. "With you around, I've had to handle myself in the shower several times." I giggle at that. "Cameron, I want to do this. It's just that I never have before, so I don't want to* do it wrong." He takes a Sharp inhale, and I am almost positive that his dick gets harder in my hand. "You do what you are comfortable with doing. Just your touch has me on fire. I doubt you could do anything to screw this up." He rasps out. So, I tighten my hand around his cock. I see precum spew out the top and wipe my thumb through it to give me some kind of lubricant. I start stroking him until there is a steady stream of precum and his breathing is heavy. His head is tipped back with his eyes closed, and he groans ever so lightly. I go a little fast, and hear his breathing speed up. I'm feeling bold, so without stopping my hand, I lean forward and lick the tip. His head comes flying forward, heat blazing in his eyes. I keep eye contact with him as I suck him into my mouth inch by agonizing inch. He moans ever so slowly, keeping full eye contact with me. "Layla, Baby, I'm not going to be able to hold off much longer." I suck hard, swirling my tongue through his slit at the same time. "Fucking hell, Baby girl. That's the fucking sexiest thing I've ever seen. But I am going to cum!!" I use my other hand to grip his balls, then deep throat his cock as far as I can take him, sucking him hard. "Oh fuck, fuck fuck I'm cumming, oh my God fuck." Cameron is spewing all kinds of slurs as I suck him dry. When I am done, I get up and head to the bathroom to wash up. I come out of the bathroom to find Cameron in the exact same spot I left him, only he is staring down at his still-hard cock.

Chapter 9

CAMERON

~

That was the most amazing experience of my life. I'm so confused as I stare at my still-hard cock. I just came harder than I ever have before, and he is still standing at attention, begging for more. I didn't even realize that Layla had come back from the bathroom until she spoke. "Did I do something wrong?" She asks. Her question was full of self-consciousness. I look up at her, bewildered by her question. She seemed unsure, and then it hit me that she admitted she had never done that before. "You did great. That was the most amazing thing I've ever felt." I try to reassure her. "But you are still hard did I not do a good enough job?" She officially looks like she is going to cry. She is within arm's reach, so I pull her to me. She is still clothed, so I pull her onto my lap so she is straddling me but not on my still hard member. I lift her chin to make sure she is looking at me. "Darlin, I'm still hard because he is a greedy bastard and wants more of you. I just came harder than I ever have before and that was all because of you! You did everything right. My dick is just wanting more that's all." I try to explain with conviction. I find myself unconsciously rubbing the pad of my thumb across her jawline for comfort. Though at this moment, I am unsure if I am trying to comfort her or myself. Because I don't want her to run from me. Especially after what we just did. I don't think I would be able to handle that, not now. "What does he want? What can I do to sate his urge?" She asks shyly. I see the redness creeping up her neck. She is embarrassed now, and she shouldn't be at all. "Layla darlin, you don't have to do anything more. I will be okay. I know you are new to all of this, and I won't push you into anything. I don't expect you to do anything more if you don't want to." I am worried about scaring her off. "Cameron, I'm not going to run from you. I feel the attraction we have. The pull, as you call it. I have never felt so close to anyone. Not even my own family would do some of the things you have done for me. I can see the fear in your eyes. But I trust you." She looks more confident now. "right now I'd like to take a bath with you. Nothing sexual. My dick can wait. But if your not going to run from me and you want to be here with me, I would like you to get used to me and be comfortable around me. Especially if these are activities you want to do together, I want you to be as comfortable as possible with us." I'm definitely going all in right now. She said she isn't running, so we will see. "Alright, but I've never been naked in front of anyone before. And you are not going to push for more..." Her blush is back, and she trails off as she looks away from me and towards the bathroom. She is fidgeting with her fingers. Showing me that she is embarrassed and nervous. But she is willing to try as long as I let her run at her pace. "Anything that does or doesn't happen while we are in there is completely up to you. I want to hold you and care for you. Anything past that, you are in complete charge of." She nods and slowly climbs off of me. "OH MY GOSH!!" she whispers and screams as she turns to me in the bathroom doorway. "What!?" I ask, looking around for something that would have caused this reaction. "We just did that, Cameron!" She whispers. "Yes, Darlin I was here for it, and it was amazing!" I whisper back. Unsure why we are whisper yelling across my room. "Cameron! Your mother is right across the *hall in the guest room!! What if she heard us!" She looks absolutely mortified. And I am now aware of why we are whisper yelling. "Layla darlin, take a breath. This room is soundproof. Has been since I bought the house." She gives me a small smile and pulls me toward the open bathroom door. I'm still half naked as I draw us a bath. All the bubbles and salts I can think to add. I Finally take my shirt off, leaving me completely nude in front of her. "Do you want to get in first, or would you like me to?" I ask cautiously. "Your already naked go ahead, and I'll start getting undressed." Her voice is breathy as she is watching me. I climb into the hot water, letting it relax my tight muscles. She gives me a small smile before she slowly starts to undress. Shirt gone, jeans gone. She is left in just her bra and underwear. My mouth has gone dry, and I just want to touch her. She looks up and sees me watching her. Her eyes went wide, and she tried to cover herself with her arms. "Don't hide yourself from me. You are pure perfection and have no reason to hide." She loosens her arms but doesn't drop them completely. After a few moments of staring at each other, she reaches back and unclasps her bra, letting it fall to the ground. I suck in a sharp inhale, which catches her attention, and whatever she sees on my face must give her a boost of confidence because she smirks at me as she ever so slowly wiggles her hips out of her panties, and they drop to pool at her feet. I start from the top and slowly rake my eyes over her curves . She just stands there, letting me take her in. I hear her giggle and snap my eyes back to hers. She is looking at my very excited member. I glance down and see the head of my dick sticking straight up out of the water and parting the bubbling I was hoping would cover this problem. I just smile at her and shake my head. "I'm not the only one happy about this." I laugh. "I'm sorry, he has a mind of his own." I shrug. Layla giggles again, and I swear I'm a goner. I anticipate her climbing in as she slowly strides toward me. Luckily, it looks as if all her self-consciousness is gone. She steps up beside the* huge tub and tests the water by swirling her hand in circles around the head of my dick. I visibly shudder at the feeling it causes, and she smirks that sexy ass smirk at me. I lift my hand out of the water for her to take so she can climb in. She takes it but surprises me as she climbs in. I assumed she would slide down in front of me between my legs, but instead, she climbed in my lap like I had her on the couch. Only all my senses are in overdrive as I can feel all of her on me. Her breasts against my chest, and her core rests on my pelvis right above my throbbing member. "Is this okay? Your breathing is a little off." She smiles, and I let out a bellowing laugh. Why am I laughing? Layla just stays there smiling at me like she won the lottery. "I'm so sorry, and I'm not used to feeling awkward or vulnerable. But you, Baby girl, make me feel like a ball of tension. I'm trying so hard not to fuck up, and you are a little minx." I chuckle. Her smile falters slightly. "I'm sorry; I'm not trying to make you feel that way." She rushes out and tries to back off my lap. "No, baby girl, don't go anywhere. You are right where you are supposed to be. And I've just never been so attracted to or felt so close to anyone like I am with you. Which makes me apparently spill everything I'm thinking. This is just as much a new feeling to me as it is to you. And I don't mind you being a minx, so please put that gorgeous smile back on your face." I was desperate for her to go back before I messed it up by laughing out my tension. "You know you let me use you earlier, right? Like you just sat there and let me use you for my own pleasure." She states. Completely taken by surprise by her outburst, I chuckle. Sliding down into the tub a little further ,she all but laying on top of me. She adjusts to be more comfortable, rubbing those gorgeous breasts against my chest as she does so. I reach up and graze my fingers on her side from her hip all the way up to the bulge of her breasts. I can feel the shiver I'm causing on her skin and the hardening of her nipples against my chest. "Why wouldn't I let you?" I finally ask her. "Well, I don't know. I wasn't helping you; I was being selfish at that moment. But you didn't care." She is whispering again. Though this time, it's breathy, almost like she can't catch her breath, and I grin, knowing that I'm causing that and all I'm doing is touching her sides. "Darlin, I would do anything for you. But you were doing it for me too. I could have gotten off when you did. But I didn't want to make a giant mess in my pants." Chuckling at the end, she gaps at me. "Layla, if you hadn't given me the head, I would have taken care of it in the shower later. I never want you to feel like you have to do things with or for me. I want you to do them because you want me." Becoming serious towards the end, she gave me a small smile. "But I did want to do that for and with you. New to me or not, I chose you and

I'm glad you enjoyed it." She is subconsciously rubbing against me, and I feel like I'm in heaven. But it's also torture. Bringing my hands down her sides, I grab hold of both sides of her hips and still her. Making eye contact, she realizes what she was doing, and the deepest shade of red covers her. "I am so sorry." She whispers. "Darlin, I am all for you wanting to use me. But as good as you feel grinding on me, it's torturing me." I sigh heavily, tipping my head back to focus on something else for a moment. "I don't want to use you, Cameron. I want you." She is moving again. Only this time, she is moving down to try to line herself up with me. I whip my head back up and grab her ass right before she tries to sink down. "Hold on there, baby girl. You've never done this before, and I'm not trying to rush you into anything." I've got her whole ass in both my hands, holding her suspended in the air right above my dick. "I know you are not Cameron. But I want this. I have never even thought about it with any of the guys I've dated before. But you, I want you, and I want you bad!" She has determination written all over her face. She breaks our eye contact as her lips come down onto my jaw and down my neck. I'm groaning and moaning. My grip on her ass gets harder the more she tempts me.

I'm in a constant shudder, trying to keep her suspended above me and trying to keep my own control. "Fine Darlin, but not in here. If you want this as much as I do. I will give you what you want. But not in here." I stand, lifting her with me. She grabs a towel off the wall hook as I carry her to the bed. I have no intention of taking her virginity tonight. I want to; everything in me wants it. I want to feel what it's like to be inside of her, to connect ourselves in that way. But even though she wants it, I don't think she is ready for that yet. I lay her down on the bed. Taking the towel from her, I glide it down her body. Slowly, making sure I get all the water. I spread her legs to dry one at a time. I am given the sight I wish I could look at for the rest of my days. I get her legs dry but never take my eyes off her pretty pussy staring back at me. She is plump and pink and already dripping out of those beautiful lips for me. Without even looking up at Layla, I toss the towel and climb on the bed between her open legs. When I am all the up where I could enter her, she takes a sharp inhale. She has now confirmed what I already knew. She isn't ready for that step, and that is completely fine. "Layla darlin, are you comfortable with me exploring you?" She let's out a breath and looks relieved. She nods and smiles, so I go forth with exploring her body. I Start with her face. "Cameron, what are you doing?" Layla giggles. I didn't tell her I was going to explore her with my mouth as well. "Exploring baby girl." I whisper into her ear before nipping it and moving on to her jaw and neck. She is so responsive to my touch, and I'm addicted to it already. I move down to her perky mounds, and they are rising and falling with Layla's heavy breathing. I do what I've been wanting to do for the last couple days. I cup one in my hand, and my goodness, does it fit so perfectly. I swipe my finger across her nipple to test her. She moans lowly and squirms a little beneath me. I grip the other one with my free hand and pull the first one in my mouth, sucking it so hard that when I let go, it makes an audible popping sound. I lean over and do the same to the other side. Layla is a groaning mess. I can tell she is trying to contain her squirming. I stay with my mouth on her voluptuous breasts as I continue my exploring with my free hand. I make it to the bottom of her stomach, and she starts to tremble. Not sure if it's good or bad, I halt my mouth exploration to look up and check to see where she is in her headspace. She looks hazy, which I like; what I don't want the wide-eyed look she's giving us. "What's wrong, baby girl? I can stop right now if you don't want to go any further." I try to reassure her that even though I'm exploring her. She is still in control of this situation. "Don't stop! Just nerves." She practically shouts at me. I smile up at her, and she returns it. I go back to my mouth assaults, but I take a moment with my roaming hand to do some reassuring rubs with my palm up and down her side until her trembling subsided. I know she is nervous, but I want her to enjoy this and not be scared. Once she stops trembling, I look back up to see her eyes closed but a smile on her face. I bring my hand back down and slowly cup her core. She takes a deep breath to calm herself, and as a reward, I bite her nipple a bit and get a small squeak from her. She opens her eyes and smiles down at me. "Are you doing okay?" I ask her before I invade her most personal space. She gives me a nod, but I don't like that. "Give me words, Layla. Are you okay with me continuing?" I ask again. "Yes" she whispers. I smile and continue. With just having my hand rest on top of her core, I can feel the heat from her radiating into my hand. I wiggle my fingers until they are between her folds, and what I find there nearly knocks the breath out of me. She is completely soaked. I mean it's so much more than when I was drying her legs. The blanket underneath her is soaked as well. I'm holding onto my resolve with thread strands now. I look up, and she won't look at me. I sit up quickly, taking her by surprise. I sit her up with me, moving her farther up the bed until she is mostly sitting with her back and head propped up by pillows. She looks at the wet spot on the bed and turns the sexy shade of red again. "Do not ever be ashamed of being turned on." The fingers I had between her folds I bring to my mouth and suck them clean. Her eyes go wide as she watches me. "You baby girl, are the most amazing thing I have ever tasted! I promise I give no fucks about this bedspread. I prefer it to smell like you anyways. But I'm going to be tasting more of you. So I gave you a better view of me while I ate that pretty little pussy of yours. The wetter you get, the more I get to have." She gasps and tries to close her legs, but I'm sitting between them, so it doesn't do her any good. "You are really going to put your mouth down there?" She stutters. "You got to taste me. Shouldn't we even the odds here?" I smirk, and she let's out a loud belly laugh. "I guess I didn't think of it that way." She states, smacking herself on the forehead. I start by kissing her from her breast all the way down. When I reach her core, I go from top to bottom, giving her kisses without entering her pretty lips. Just letting her get used to me being down here. After I'm done, I look up and keep my eyes locked on hers as I take my tongue out and run it through her folds. She shudders under me, and her eyes become hooded. I bring my hand over to gently rub circles on her clit as I continue to dig my tongue in further to taste more and more of her. Never breaking eye contact with Layla. She watches me, her breath getting faster. I switch my approach as I can see she is getting close. I take my middle finger down through her fold to get it nice and lubed up. I take her little bud in my mouth, sucking and licking, and when I think she is close to tipping over that edge. I

slide my finger into her pussy, bending it up slightly to hit just the right spot. Within seconds, Layla is yelling my name and squirting all over me. Well, that's new. But fuck if I'm going to complain about it. I keep my finger inside her. I love how she feels around me. But I can't get enough of the feeling of her aftershock pulses that try to strangle my finger. I keep licking until there is nothing left. Finally, I slide my *finger out of her. I look up at her, and she looks exhausted. I grab one of my shirts and pull it over her head. Layla gives me a sleepy smile. "Sleep darlin, you have work in the morning." I whisper before kissing her on the head. I go to the closet and get her a new blanket, then head to the shower to clean up quickly. The blue balls I have right now are beyond worth it. Finding out she was a squirter was a bit surprising. However, I assume she didn't know. I am replaying this whole evening in my head as I release the pent-up tension inside me. It is definitely not the same as having Layla's mouth on me, but it will have to do for now. After calming myself a few times, I climbed out of the shower and toweled off. I throw on a pair of boxers and climb into bed beside Layla.*

LAYLA

I woke up to my alarm blaring. I go to roll over to grab my phone but can't. I am currently completely tangled in a mess of arms and legs with Cameron. I try to peel my limbs from his. Though it seems every time I try, his grip on me tightens. I slightly shake his arm, trying to wake him enough so that I can get untangled. After shaking his arm a few times, he sleepily opens his eyes. He smiles brightly at me before taking in the sound of my alarm. He squints to see the clock on his dresser and then sighs, letting me free. Once I successfully shut off my alarm. I feel his arm wrap back around me, pulling me back into him. I giggle and try to wiggle away, but he isn't letting me go. He turned me till I was facing him and he pressed a feather-like kiss on my forehead. "Good morning, Darlin." He rasps out. "Good morning, Cameron." I whispered, getting lost in his eyes. We lay there just taking in the moment. When I suddenly come back to my senses, realizing I need to get ready for work. I have been dreading this day since Friday. I pull away from Cameron, not missing the disappointment in his eyes. "I have to get ready for work." I state flatly, making sure he knows that I, too, am disappointed we had to cut this short. "Do you mind if I join you in the shower?" He asks. I can see the hope hanging in his eyes. I just raise an eyebrow. "Nothing sexual, I promise. I just want to take care of you, that's all." He looks like a puppy begging for attention. So, I Crack a grin and agree. He does exactly as he promises. Taking care of all of me. He digs his fingers into my scalp gently ,massages the shampoo in and rinses it out the same way. Grabbing a loofah and soaping it up, he runs it all over my body until he is sure I'm clean from head to toe. He rinses me in the same manner. I try to help wash him, but he bats my hands away with a grin. He then rushes through washing himself. And I don't think I have ever felt more appreciated than I do right now. Cameron grabs a towel and completely dries me. Walking to the closet, I grab clothes and put them on. Walking back into the room, Cameron is already dressed and waiting for me. I'm taken aback by the look on his face. "What? Do I look bad?" I panicked. His features soften immediately. "No, not at all. I guess I just didn't expect you to wear your old clothes when we just got you a bunch of new clothes." He states. "I would love to wear my new clothes. But I get so dirty at work I don't want to ruin any of my new stuff." I state sadly. Understanding sweeps across his face, and he looks guilty. "I'm sorry! I completely forgot how dirty it gets in that factory. Can I drive you to work?" His eyes are pleading with me. "That's fine. But can we take your least flashy vehicle?" He is looking at me like I slapped him. "Cameron, it isn't personal. I'm just not trying to draw attention to myself, and your flashy cars will definitely do that! I don't even know if I still have my job. What if I get there and they tell me I'm fired. I won't be able to leave." I'm starting to freak out a little bit. Cameron reaches for me and pulls me into a hug. I take a deep breath. I breathe him in and calm immediately as he rubs soothing circles on my back. "I doubt they have fired you. But you have my number, and if

anything happens, you call me immediately, and I will come get you."
Giving me a no-nonsense look. I breathe out an alright as we start
walking downstairs to get breakfast. His mother's door is still closed,
so I assume she is still sleeping. But it is 5am. If I didn't have to work, I
would still be sleeping. In the kitchen, I pour both Cameron, and I
coffee and make a place at the counter for us while he makes some
scrambled eggs and bacon quick. After finishing Breakfast, we get into
Cameron's least flashy car. Which is the SUV we went shopping in
yesterday. I felt like face-palming myself when we pulled up. Several
people walking up to the building slowed their pace to gawk. "Look at
me darlin." I turn to face Cameron. He pulls me over the center consul
and into his lap. Luckily, these windows are tinted. Although I'm sure
it's not enough for this interaction. "Eyes on me, baby girl. No one else
here matters." I'm drowning in his dark eyes as he runs his fingers
lightly up and down my thighs. Then, before I could even think of
anything to say. He pulls me into a toe-curling kiss. Right here in the
parking lot of my work. And as soon as his lips hit mine, I completely
forgot where I was at. Things started to get heated. Cameron pulled
away slowly, and all at once, I remembered where I was. This time, I
really did face-palm myself. Cameron just chuckles and let's me climb
back into my seat. He leaned over and gave me a light, sweet kiss to
the temple. I open the door to get out. Grabbing my hand, he says,
"Remember, you need me for anything you call, and I will be here." I
nod shyly ,step down from the SUV and walk inside. I get a few side
glances, but they look away as soon as I catch them. It's not that I am
ashamed of Cameron. Not at all. It's that I don't want people to think
that I am trying to sleep my way to the top. I have earned everything
I have had, and that's what I want to be known for.

Chapter 10

LAYLA

As I walk in and move around the locker room. I feel someone staring at me. I looked in the direction to find the girl I thought to be my best friend. Leah stands there staring at me with what looks like a scowl on her face. She seems so entranced that she doesn't seem to notice that I see her. I clear my throat, and she seems to snap out of it. Her eyes went wide for half a second before she pulled herself back together. She walks over, smiling at me like nothing had happened. "Layla, I'm so happy to see you! I heard your apartment got broken into. Is everything okay?" She asks with what I can now see as fake concern. The funny thing is, this is how she has always talked to me. I am starting to feel like this whole friendship has been fake. "Yes, my apartment was broken into, and all of my belongings were completely destroyed. Luckily, I wasn't home, so I wasn't personally harmed by whoever it was that did it." I say, trying to keep my tone even. She doesn't seem to know that I have caught on to her bogus concern. I'm breaking inside though, I thought that we were friends and that even with her leaving me on Friday, she would apologize or something. But right now, standing in front of her, she looks like a snake wearing sheep's wool. She didn't apologize for Friday, and she knew about my apartment, though she never called or texted me at all to see if I was okay or needed anything. She was the only real friend I had here. I go to walk away when she stops me. "I saw you being dropped off this morning. That's a nice SUV, I must have finally given up that V card for a ride like that. Hmm? She quirks any eyebrow up, waiting for a response. But instead, I just roll my eyes and walk off. Heading to my area I see several eyes on me. It's pretty nerve-wracking, but I do what Cameron said and decide that no one else matters; I'm just here to do my job. It's about 9:30, and my team lead comes to fetch me. Says HR wants to talk to me. Oh goodie. I head up to the front offices to see HR. Once I get there, I found not only HR but also our plant manager. "Ms. Nichols, please have a seat," Jeff said gruffly. "It has been brought to our attention that you are sleeping with Cameron Magnolia. And even though his company funds our facility, we can't allow you to work here. While being in a relationship, no matter the type, with someone so influential in our company." He states, staring at me in disgust. I am so shell-shocked by this that I am just sitting there staring at him. Before I even get the chance to tell them I'm not sleeping with him.

HR hands me a paper summing up my termination. I grab it, feeling ambushed. I turn and walk out of the office without saying a word. I get to my locker and grab my phone. I dial Cameron. He picks up on the second ring. I hear people talking in the background and realize I called him while in a meeting. "What's wrong darlin." He asks. I break down and just start crying. "Grab everything you need I am on my way." There was no hesitation nor anger in his voice. I pull myself together and pack up my locker. I am walking out as Leah comes walking into the locker room. She looks smug but hides it quickly. "Oh my gosh, Layla. Did they really fire you for staring at Cameron on Friday? That's absolutely absurd!" She is trying to sound upset to me. But all I catch is that she knows who Cameron is and what he looks like. Which means she likely saw him at the club Friday night. Something is off with her and this situation. But I'm to upset right now to focus on her. I just sidestepped her and continued my journey outside to wait for Cameron.

CAMERON

I am sitting in the middle of a meeting, and my phone goes off. I don't usually have my phone during staff meetings, but I wanted to make sure if Layla needed me, I was there. When I glance over at it, sure enough, her name pops up, and I answer right away. "What's wrong darlin?" I ask. At first, she is quiet, and then she bursts into tears. I am instantly pissed at what could have caused this. "Grab everything you need I am on my way." I use the softest voice I can muster up, with rage flying through me. At this point, everyone in the meeting is staring at me. "Please forgive me I have somewhere important I need to be. Please continue, if someone can take notes, I will gladly review them later. Thank you." I stand from my seat and make my way out quickly . I don't know what happened, but my girl is upset, and I have to get to her. I pull into the parking lot 10 mins later to find her sitting on the sidewalk. She has her head held high as people come and go, staring at her. I park at the curb and get out. As soon as I leave the cover of my SUV everyone stops and stares. I walk around the car and kneel on the ground in front of her. She looks me straight in the eye and says, "They fired me. Some one told them I was sleeping with you. They told me that even though our company is reliant on you, it is seen as unprofessional to be sleeping with you. They didn't even let me say anything; just handed me my papers. I knew I didn't like that guy Jeff." She is muttering to herself I think more than me. I grab her stuff and put it in the SUV. I turn back to her and take her by the hand, helping her up. I can see the hurt in her eyes even though she is trying to keep it together on the outside. I place a soft kiss on her forehead and walk her to the passenger side. Once she is seated, I tell her to stay in the car I would be right back. She isn't looking at me now, just nodding. I close the door and head into the building. Everyone stops and stares as I walk through the office to find our good friend Jeff. I spot him still in the HR office. He was laughing with the HR team, that is, until his eyes met me. Fear floods his face as he goes completely pale. "Mr. Magnolia, what a surprise. We were not expecting you today." He stutters, getting to his feet. "Well, you see Jeff I wasn't planning to have to come in today either." I state as I close the door behind me. "Well, um what can we do for you today Sir?" He is still sputtering over his words. "Well, you see Jeff, I have the most beautiful young lady sitting out in my SUV, waiting for me to take her back to my house as she tries to put her life back together for the second time in the last few days. So here is the deal. You don't want her to work for you because she is staying with me that's fine. But let's get something straight.

You will tell me who informed you that she and I are sleeping together. Once we have established who thinks it's necessary to be in other people's business, we will then get down to whether or not I re-sign your contract. So, who was it!" I am completely raging on the inside. However, I did my best to keep my tone as neutral as possible. Jeff does as he was told.

He told me who informed HR of the information, and I then told him I was not going to re-sign our contract. He was completely distraught by the news and, by the end, was begging for me to re-sign. I clearly stated that the actions taken by his team were not in line with my ethics and how we run businesses. He should have done what he could to find the truth of the accusation before bluntly accusing and terminating the employee. This drop is his own doing. Adjusting my suit jacket, I opened the door and walked out. There is now a crowd outside the office. I breeze through the crowd and out the door. Jeff can handle giving the news. I slide into the driver's seat and see that my baby girl was crying while I was gone, and she is now asleep. I slide her seat belt around her sleeping form and then take off toward home.

LAYLA

I wake up in bed. I have no idea how long I was asleep, but when I opened my eyes, I saw Cameron laying beside me, typing on his phone. Quite aggressively, might I add. He looks pissed, and honestly, I'm not sure if I want to interrupt him or pretend like I'm still sleeping. He finally glances my way and sees me looking at him. His face softens immediately. "How are you feeling darlin?" He asks, setting his phone on the nightstand. I just shrug, honestly I'm not sure how I am right now. He slides over and pulls me to him.

Lifting me till I'm sitting on his lap, face to face. "I have something to tell you. And you are not going to like it. Do you want me to tell you now, or would you like to go soak in the tub with me for a bit before?" He is talking so gently, like he might spook a wild animal. I lean forward and rest my forehead against his. "It was Leah wasn't it?" I ask with my eyes closed. Letting out a deep breath, he says, "Yes, baby girl, yes it was, I am so sorry. I made Jeff tell me who told them we were sleeping together. He said that she came in early and told them first thing this morning. But you sound like you already knew." He says, but it sounds more like a question. "Yeah, I wasn't completely sure, nor did I want to believe it. But once you said that, I knew. I knew it was her. She was off today when I was around her. I caught her scowling at me, I think. Then she brought up my apartment, asking if I was okay. Though she never messaged me over the weekend. She seemed almost smug when I passed her as I was leaving the building. I just don't know why." I whisper all this to him while silent tears slip down my cheeks. Stroking my hair, I feel his breath as he promises *that he will help me figure out why this is happening. Pulling me into a hug. He leans forward and wraps my legs and arms around him. He picks me up with him off the bed and into the bathroom. Sitting me on the counter, he draws us a bath. I am feeling delirious now as I just start laughing. Cameron swings around, confused by my laughter. "What is so funny, baby girl?" I just grin. "I was just thinking about how good of a bath this is going to be." I'm still laughing, and he is still confused. "The water is so hot it's steaming. And my muscles could really use that right now." To me, this makes complete sense, but Cameron still seems confused. So I climbeded off the counter and just started taking my clothes off. His face heats, and his eyes darken. I can see the want and desire written all over him. But if there is anything I feel with the man in front of me, it is safe. Cameron has had several opportunities to take advantage of me if he wanted to. Not once has he ever done anything with out permission. So, instead of feeling scared as he watches me undress, I feel the spark of desire that makes me feel bold and alive. Just like the night before. I walk up to him, in all my naked glory and raise my hand for him to help me into the tub. He is stuck in place till I clear my throat. He blinks back to reality and helps me into the tub. As if waiting for permission to join, he just stands there with puppy dog eyes. "Are you going to just stand there? Or are you going to join me?" I ask him. Once given the okay he was looking for. He frantically starts stripping his clothes off. The water sloshes around me as he enters the tub behind me. After he gets settled where he wants, he pulls me back against him, my back to his front. "Can I touch you? Nothing sexual if you don't want. I just want to be able to touch you." He asks hesitantly. "Yes sweets, I want you to touch me." I say as certain as I can. He reaches in front of me, grabbing a wash rag I didn't even see hanging there. He sets it on my knee, then brings his hands up my stomach, around my breasts, up my side. Looping his fingers through my hair ,he lightly pulls it all behind me and into the waiting water. He slowly adds water to my hair rinsing away the shit storm of today. Because I can no longer think of anything other than how wonderful it feels to have his fingers massaging my scalp. I lay back against him and let him care for me in a way I don't think I have ever cared for myself. Cameron seems to know what I need at this moment, more then I do. I must have fallen asleep again because the next thing I know, I am being lifted out of the tub. I snuggle into Cameron as the cool air hits me as we leave the bathroom. "Don't you have work you need to be doing?" I ask him, knowing that he left work to come get me. And has been with me ever since. "I do, but making sure you are okay has taken priority at the moment. Plus, I have an office here that I can work from. Let's get dried off and dressed. Once we are decent, we will go down and grab lunch. After that, and as long as you are feeling okay, I will head to my office to get some work done." He says. I just nod and start drying off. He goes into the walk-in and grabs clothes for both of us before coming back out. Handing me my clothes, he lays a gentle kiss on my forehead and then starts getting dressed. I blush a deep red at the gesture but turn and get dressed. I didn't realize how hungry I was until he mentioned food. I checked the clock and saw that it was 1 pm. No wonder I feel like I'm starving. "Come, baby girl, let's get some food." He whispers, brushing my hair out of my face. He takes my hand in his, enters, lacing our fingers. I glance down because the tingles and everything else just feel so right and so calming. Even in the shit storm that is currently taking over my life. I look up to meet his eyes, and he looks worried. "what's the matter, sweets?" I ask him softly. "Did I do something wrong? Do you not want to hold hands? We don't have to let people know that we are together. Wait, are we together? I am so sorry! I am rambling." He looks so adorable right now. But he's right, are we together? Hands still locked, I drag him to the couch and pull him down onto it with me. "Cameron, I was just thinking about how much I enjoy the tingles we share and how our hands fit together. I was thinking how right it felt even with my life completely falling apart. And if we are together, I'm not ashamed of people knowing that." I reassure him. He physically relaxes and pulls me to him. "Can we be together? Will you date me?" He asks with a big, goofy grin on his face. I sit for a minute and take in my situation and everything I have been through since I moved out here. Not one time since I have moved away from home,*

have I felt as safe and happy as I do when I am with Cameron. I must be taking too long because when I meet his eyes again, they have dimmed. I now feel like an asshole for taking a moment. But I just smile brightly at him and say, "Yes!" I'm being carried again. Only this time, it's over his shoulder. Out of his room, down the hall, the steps and into the kitchen. I can feel eyes on me as I stop fighting him on the stairs, so I am just hanging like a dead weight. Once in the kitchen, he flings me back upright and sets me on the kitchen island. It takes me a minute to get my bearings and shake off the whiplash I've been given. Standing at the stove is a lady in her 30s maybe, she had her back to me at first. As we walked into the kitchen, I couldn't see anything, but I heard Cameron greet someone. I am scowling at a smiling Cameron when the girl turns from the stove to face us. She seemed pleasant as she turned to look at Cameron and then startled when her eyes found me sitting atop the island. I smile at her, but she doesn't greet me. Just turns back to Cameron, trying to grab his attention. "Mr. Magnolia, would you like a late lunch, sir? I can prepare something quick." Her tone is sickly sweet. Like one of those girls that are trying to get a guy's attention way too hard, and you want to gag. I do my best to hold back mine. It doesn't go unnoticed though, because Cameron isn't even listening to her; he is still watching me. He gives me a puzzled look. He is oblivious to this girl right now. Luckily, his mother takes this as a perfect opportunity to cut in. I didn't even see her at the table. Her eyes must have been the ones I felt on me when we walked in. "Layla honey, so good to see you! How are you doing? Cameron told me what happened this morning. But don't you worry! We are handling it." She is talking as she walks up and gives me a warm hug, shoving her son out of the way a bit as she does. He groans with disapproval, but she only winks at him. After she let's go of me. Cameron is instantly in front of me again. "Wendy, please get lunch for both Layla and me. We will be in my office. Mother, are you staying another night, or are you heading home today?" He asks, never looking away from me. I can feel Wendy's heated stare hitting the side of my face when I hear Mrs. Magnolia speak up. "Oh dear, it seems we are going to have an issue here." She says, quite sternly. "Wendy, I think maybe you should go until you can understand that just because you work in this house doesn't mean that my son is interested in you." Everything has become quite tense now. You can cut it with a knife, and my dear Cameron is lost, to say the least. "Mother, why would you tell her to leave? She works here, and she knows that I am not into her. I've never had any interaction with her other than professionally." He says, still confused. "Well dear boy, because she is always trying to flirt with you. She just did it a few moments ago, and poor Layla had to keep from gagging at the overly sweet tone she used to talk to you. And considering the daggers she was throwing Layla's way moments ago, I would say she doesn't understand that all of your interactions have been nothing but professional." She sighs at the end like she is annoyed he hasn't noticed. Turning to Wendy, Cameron finally gives her his full attention. "Is this true? You think that I am into you?" He questions her. "Well sir, I am the only younger lady that works here. All the others are older, and you never bring any other girls here. So I thought..." Wendy trails off as reality sinks in. "I am so sorry, and I didn't mean to overstep." She rushes out. "Where you really throwing daggers at Layla?" He questions her again. "Of course not, sir!" she lies. "So I am lying?" His mother cuts in. "No ma'am. I just.." The poor girl is humiliated. "Stop. Please everyone, just stop." I cut in. "Listen, Wendy, I don't at all blame you for wanting him to like you. Good God look at him." I chuckle, trying to lighten the mood. "However, has he ever done anything to make you think he liked you other than you being the only younger worker?" I ask. "No." she states. "But he must really like you because you are the only girl I have ever seen here. Other than his mother. I'm sorry I didn't mean to be rude. I got jealous over something I had no right to be jealous of. I was startled to see you when I turned around." She looks utterly ashamed, and I feel bad. I originally thought she was going to be a problem also, but she seems genuinely sorry. "I do really like her. And she is mine and will be staying here. So if this is going to be a problem, then we need to handle it now." Cameron states. Shaking her head, she says, "No sir, I understand now. Please accept my apology to all of you." Everyone accepts and Wendy starts making food. "I think I will stay until we figure out what is happening with Layla and all the people out to get her." His mother states. "Let's take this to my office." Cameron says, and then he picks me up, wraps me around him like a child and walks off as his mother laughs behind us.

CAMERON

I was so confused in the kitchen. I had never noticed the way that Wendy had acted around me. I guess since I wasn't really into any girls, I just never paid that much attention to her or her behavior. However I definitely would not stand for her to be jealous and try to do something to my girl. We reached my office, and I felt a seriousness hit my chest. I'm pulled into my own thoughts of five years ago, losing my dad and brother. I know that I am still carrying my baby girl, but other than feeling our tingles, I am lost in my own head. Walking to my chair, I sit down, Layla still with me. "What's the matter, Sweets?" She asks. I don't get a chance to answer before my mom does. "Get out of your head, boy! This situation isn't the same. I know where you are at, and it's never a good place to be." She states in a do it or do-it-or-else tone. I stretch and rub a hand down my face, bringing myself back to the present. "What's happening?" Layla asks cautiously. "Your situation, baby girl is similar to the one that got my father and brother killed." I state bluntly. I can feel her shudder, then go visibly pale. Leaning forward, I place my hands on each side of her face and my forehead on hers. "I will NEVER let anything happen to you!" I take slow, measured breaths to try to calm myself as flashbacks flood my mind. I was in the car that night. I saw both of them die in front of me, and there was nothing I could do to help them. Silent tears run down my face. I didn't even realize I was crying until I felt tingles wipe them away. "I'm so sorry what you guys have had to go through. I don't want to be the one to bring up bad memories." She says quietly but loud enough for my mother to hear. "Oh honey, the memories, good and bad, plague us every day. This is not your fault." Her voice is shaky, and I glance over to see her crying as well. I know my mother is strong, though I also know she suffers being alone all the time. "Well, Cameron, we need to tell her. I know you don't want to, and honestly, neither do I. But she means the world to you; that's clear to see. So I don't see her going anywhere, and we need to get to the bottom of what is happening to her if we want to keep her." My mother sounds determined to get through this, so let's go.

Chapter 11

CAMERON

"Where do we start?" I ask my mother. "From the beginning Love." She says quietly. " About a year before they died, my father had made a deal. He signed this contract with another local businessman. For your safety, I will not tell you who. All you need to know is that my father thought that it was a safe and legit contract. My father was a man of humility; he treated others with respect and always tried to do the right thing. Needless to say, when he found out that his now partner was doing illegal activities under the contract that he was bound to, He confronted the man. Told him that wasn't the type of thing he dealt in. My father told the man to stop, or he would turn him in. Obviously, his partner didn't take that kindly. Told my father it wouldn't be a smart move on his part to turn him in. You see, we found out later that their plan all along was to make my dad look like a corrupt man. They wanted everything my family had. One of my father's former business partners from years past came forward after the accident. He was a greedy man and cared for no one but himself and whom he could crush to get what he wanted. So he teamed up with This man who had tricked my father. Back then, you had to have solid evidence if you wanted to put someone behind bars, especially someone like this guy." I pause and look over at my mother to see how she is doing. Her eyes are shut, but her leg is bouncing, so I know she is still with us. Sighing, I continue. "It only took about a week before they started following my father everywhere. I can only assume they were tipped off that my father was gathering evidence to present to the police. One night my father, my brother and I had gone out to dinner. We were on our way home when some car came crashing into us from behind. The car started spinning in all directions. My father tried to stop, but they had tampered with our brakes ahead of time, so there was nothing he could do." I am officially crying, and so is my mother. I can hear her sniffling. "You don't have to continue, Cameron. I can see how hard this is for both of you." She says gently. "No darlin, you need to understand the loss we have suffered to know the lengths we will go to for you." I say. "We ended up in a tall ditch upside down. I can't remember how many times we flipped. I think I blacked out for a bit. When I came to, both my father and brother were dead. I have no idea how long I was in that car with them before help arrived. It was a horrific scene that I will unfortunately never unsee. But I learned a lot that day. First thing, trust no one. Two, if you do trust, make sure you have been given several reasons that make that person trustworthy. And three, Never take anything for granted." I sit back and wait. For what, I'm not sure. Though this is the moment that Wendy takes to bring our lunch into us. I'm grateful for the distraction, and it was nice being able to tell that to someone. We haven't trusted anyone in the last 5 years. Pretty much everyone still thinks it was a freak accident. After Wendy leaves the room, Layla speaks. "Do the Police know what happened? Like what really happened." I sigh, "Yes, they do. But there wasn't enough hard evidence to work with, only conspiracies. My father's old business partner came forward, and he ended up missing. Paid off to shut up, or just completely taken out like my father and brother? We will likely never know. So, it has just gone unsolved. And unfortunately, for our own safety, we have had to let it stay that way. Since we dropped everything, we have been left alone, with no contact or any sign of them." Pausing, I then say, "That's why, *until right now, we have not told anyone the truth of what actually happened to them. One, it is hard to trust anyone. Second, for our own safety, Don't get me wrong Layla, we have since done everything possible to keep ourselves protected. We have made friends with people some wouldn't, in order to be prepared for in case they do come back."* I sit in silence, waiting for her to take in everything that has been thrown into the open. *"The point of us telling you this honey is so you know that we will do everything in our power to make sure that you are okay. Nothing will keep us from finding out what is happening to you and why. We will keep you safe."* my mother says, cutting in. Layla just nods, still trying to take in all the information. *"Everything you both have been through sounds like complete Hell! Excuse my language."* She says shyly, glancing at my mom. Mother just chuckles and waves her off. *"Layla darlin, if you want us to help, we need to know everything that has happened."* I say gently.

LAYLA

Ugh they want to know everything. I am feeling really embarrassed right now.

Because not only did I just realize that I had to tell them both about my past failures. But I also never told Cameron about my family, or lack there of, back home. I sigh but nod in agreement. I climb from Cameron's lap to head to the sofa beside the chair his mother is sitting in. Cameron doesn't hesitate to join me on the sofa. *"My story is uncomfortable to tell, probably mainly for me."* I chuckle, but it's dry without actual humor. Cameron squeezes me to his side. *Well, here goes nothing.* *"I'm not from here originally. Which is probably pretty obvious. I grew up in a small town in Arkansas. My father owned his own construction company. Nothing big or fancy, but he enjoyed it. My mother, on the other hand, was my best friend. My father wanted me to take over his business someday. So he wanted me to go to college for business. That was never my passion. I wanted to be part of the process, and I love the architecture of the build. But he didn't understand. My mother did! She always encouraged me to be me. But the cancer in her brain took her from me in her junior year of high school. My father just couldn't cope with the loss. Picked up drinking a lot. He became verbally abusive. I just kept my head down and pushed myself a senior year to get out. And I did; I got a full-ride scholarship to the University of Nevada. Needless to say, he was very upset. That night, after he passed out drunk, I packed all I could and left. I got here, settled into my dorm and started my 1st term. I didn't have money, so I picked up 2 part-time jobs. It wasn't long before some kid who went to the same school was hitting on me. We hung out a few times. But same as with Roman, I didn't want to sleep with him. Which should be no big deal; we are on a campus full of sluts; take your pick and leave me be, right? But no, he got pissed, and that's when I found out his father was the Dean. The next thing I knew, I was being thrown out of the dorms and college. So I packed up again and lived out of a hotel for a few weeks till I was able to save enough money to get the flat I had. Before someone ruined the whole thing." I thought that by telling this story, I would be an emotional wreck. Crying and sorts, but it's made me angry. Angry for all the things I have gone through for absolutely no reason. And not having a welcoming home back in Arkansas to go to for help. As I am taking deep breaths to try and calm down because I had worked myself up pretty well. Cameron asks, "So you never got to finish college?" I take a deep breath, "No, I made it through the first two semesters without being noticed. I got good grades, went to work, studied. Then everything went wrong." I just shrug. "Could any of this be linked to all of that?" Mrs. Magnolia asks. "I doubt it; that was over 3 years ago now." I say. "You haven't been home or talked to your father in 3 years." Cameron asks. The pang of guilt I feel knowing that he would likely do anything to see or even just talk to his father. "No, it's not that I don't want to. I love my father, but the last time I saw him, he was extremely drunk. When I told him I was leaving to study architecture, he screamed at me. Told me if I left not to bother coming back because I wouldn't be welcome." I wipe a tear that makes its way down my cheek. "So, you couldn't follow your passion. And three years ago, you got a job at that factory to get back on your feet, all by yourself. And that company just fired you over some bullshit rumor that wasn't even completely true!" Cameron now seems to be seething. "Yes." This is the only reply I can come up with. "Well, that makes me feel better about It then." He states triumphantly. "Better about what?" His mother asks. "That I told him I wasn't going to renew our contract. Because the way we run a business doesn't coincide with the way he is running his facility," He states proudly. I didn't know this; I knew he went inside, and I knew he found out that Leah was the one that lied about me. But I didn't know this! "Cameron, are you sure that was a good idea?" His mother asks. "Why not? I didn't do anything wrong. Whether the situation had to do with Layla or not. That is not how we conduct our businesses. We do not treat our employees that way. There should have been a fair investigation into the allegations. Then, from there, they should have taken action based on the evidence found in the investigation." He states firmly. "It's not your ethics. I am questioning love. But what if they are in on what is happening to Layla? Maybe we should have kept them close and then restructured management later." His mother is smart. "I never would have thought of that." I say quietly. I wouldn't think there were so many people out to get me. For what? I'm not an important person; I don't come from a big background. But we have to start somewhere, and right now, the only two people out to get me are Roman and my ex-best friend Leah.*

"So where do we start?" I ask.

Chapter 12

CAMERON

~

My mother is right, I didn't think of the people at the factory being in on everything either. I was just angry about the way they treated her. "I know you don't think that the situation with the college isn't part of this, but just to be sure, I will be calling in some favors to have it silently looked into." I say to Layla. "Are you calling Ace?" My mother asks. "Yes, he will know exactly how to go about this." I say. I look down at Layla to gauge how she is feeling about everything. But she is just staring off like she has spaced completely out of our conversation. "Layla, Darlin, are you okay?" I ask gently. She jumps slightly when I grab her hand. "Yes, I'm fine, just taking everything in. How terrible things have been for you both and how did I get into this mess to begin with? I

feel like an asshole for judging you that first night. I feel so bad. I laughed in your face because I didn't believe you! And you have gone out of your way to keep me safe and now to find out who is doing this to me, and I am a bit overwhelmed." She is crying now. I slowly wipe her tears and hold her tighter till she calms down. "Darlin, I am not even the slightest bit upset about what happened before. You didn't know me then, and all you had to go off of were rumors. I was hurt at the time, but not by you. By the fact that I had hidden myself away for so long that people thought that low of me." It's true. I may have been upset then, but all it has shown me is that I clearly need to make more appearances. *Don't get me wrong, I donate to a lot of charities, and I am a kind person. But I never go to the charity balls that they throw in honor. I always thought it was cliché. But now I realize that no one knows the real me. The only good thing about the situation right now is that I can use the current perception people have of me to use in helping to protect Layla. Sliding off the couch, I grab the throw from the back and wrap Layla in it. I walk to my desk and have a seat. I take a couple of deep breaths to calm my nerves. Ace is a good guy, don't get me wrong. But he is the club leader of a biker gang outside of town. We are what I would like to call friends, though this is the first time I have had to call him for help. I grab my phone and click on his name. The phone rings a couple of times before Ace answers. "Long time since I've seen your name on my screen Cameron. What's wrong, my friend?" He doesn't even bother with pleasantries. "I need your help Ace." I state rougher than I wanted to. "Are you home?" He asks. "Yes." I say. "I'm on my way. We will talk soon." And then the call ends. "Ace is on his way. We will fill him in when he arrives." I say, relaxing a bit. "He is coming Here?" Layla asks. "Yes, Ace doesn't trust conversations over the phone. That's why our call was so short, and nothing important was said. When he gets here though, I need you to understand that he is a pretty scary guy. He is the club leader for a biker gang outside of town. However, he is a good guy, one that I consider a friend. He is here to help." She still looks worried, but there isn't much more I can do right now.*

LAYLA

I am feeling pretty numb. The amount of information that has been brought to light in the last hour or so, Has been a lot on both sides. I was intrigued by the guy named Ace, who was supposed to be here anytime. After the call that Cameron made to him, we all kind of sat in the silence of the room eating our very late lunch. I think the heaviness of having to tell this other person I don't know about everything is what frightens me more than knowing who he is. But if he is here to help, I will tough it out. There is a knock on the door of the office. "Come In" Cameron's voice booms through the office. A man around Cameron's age walks in. He is tall and covered in Tattoos from what I can see anyways. He is wearing nice jeans and a tank top under the leather vest full of patches. His eyes sweep the room as if a natural instinct. His eyes catch mine, and he stops mid-stride. I can't tell if he is confused or intrigued. Most likely both. His hair is long on top and buzzed on the sides. He is very tall, so I can see where Cameron would think I would find him intimidating. He not once pulls his attention from me until what I can only describe as a growl of disapproval comes from Cameron. Ace's head whips straight to meet Cameron, who is standing now behind his desk. Looking back at me one more time, he continues to walk to greet Cameron. "Cameron, who is the girl?" Ace asks bluntly. "That Ace is Layla. And she is why you're here friend." Cameron says with a smirk. He knew that dirty dog knew that Ace was going to hit on me. Ace walks to me and sits at the opposite end of the sofa. He isn't touching me or going out of his way to be flirty. But I can see the mischief in his eyes. "Layla, did you know. That in all the years I have known Cameron. I have never once seen a woman in this house other than his lovely mother." Throwing her a wink, she waves off with a smile. "Or the staff that work here. That, my dear tells me a lot. However, growling at me in disapproval. Well, that is new." He is laughing now. "Are you done making fun of him for picking me? I thought you were coming here to help." I say, annoyed by his drawn out one sided banter. "Feisty, I like it. Since I took it, you're the one with the problem. And a decent one since I have been called. Feisty is what we are going to need." He taps my foot and then turns his attention to Cameron. Leaving his desk, Cameron comes over to the sofa, lifting me and setting me back down on his lap. He adjusts the throw blanket back over me. I here Ace, trying to hold back his laughter at Cameron's pampering. "Alright so we need your help. Someone is after Layla. I am almost positive that this has been a long-term scheme. Though we only know of two people that are involved." Cameron was kind enough to go through everything with Ace as I just sat there and winced at the bad parts. Once finished, I snuck a peek at Ace because, just like always, I feel like this story makes me seem pretty pathetic, and I'm feeling really small in front of this huge tattoo-covered tough guy. But when I look at him, he looks pained. I can read his eyes, but when they lock with mine, the anger in them is overwhelming. I shrink back into Cameron on instinct. "He isn't angry at you, baby girl. Let's just say that Ace has had to deal with people like this before. That is why I called him for help." He whispered. "We start at the college. I am in agreement with the fact that this all began there. I don't know how these other two jokers fit in, but there is a connection somewhere." Ace's voice is straining to keep his composure. We stay in the office for a while longer. Mrs. Magnolia has gone off to bed as Cameron and Ace form a plan. We are leaving most of the heavy work to Ace and his guys, as they don't want me getting anywhere near the people who are trying to get me. I had been so upset and frustrated about how everything in my life was going wrong. That I didn't even realize until now the amount of actual danger I have been in. Especially with Leah being my friend, she could have been trying to set me up this whole time. "Do you think that last Friday, Leah was trying to set me up? Like you saw her leave me at the club drunk and alone. What if Roman was there at the club. But you got to me first? What if he thought you would take me home? So he waited awhile, and that's when he broke into my flat. But got angry I wasn't there and destroyed all my stuff." My mind is finally putting all the pieces together. I have been wallowing and not paying attention to everything that has happened. I am a smart girl, but the disarray of my life recently had me spiraling. "I think that very well could be what happened. And Loverboy here luckily couldn't leave you alone long enough to let anything happen to you." Ace says, half playful, half serious. "Has she tried to contact you since this morning when you were fired?" Cameron asks. "Honestly, I don't know. I haven't had my phone. I think it's in your room on the nightstand." I say. Cameron stands to leave the office to go get my phone. Glancing back at me to make sure I feel okay being alone with Ace. I nod, and he continues out the door. "You mean a lot to him. I can see it in the way he looks at you. That man loves you and has only known you for 4 days. Impressive, since he never paid any mind to most women. What is it about you that has captured my friend so strongly." Ace has a twinkle of pure curiosity in his eyes. "I don't know. We just have a really strong connection to each other. Have you ever felt when someone was watching you? Not in a creepy way or anything. But just like the comfort of knowing they are there and paying attention. It's odd, and it's stronger when we touch. It leaves tingles everywhere there is skin-to-skin contact. I don't know what it is or why it chose him and I. But I know that there was only one other person that made me feel as safe as I do with him, and that was my mother before she died. So, If the way he feels for me feels like that, and that is what love feels and looks like. Then I probably love him to." At that very moment, Cameron, steps into the room. He heard me. It's written all over his face. I look over at Ace, and he is smiling widely at me. I glare at him, and his whole belly laughs. Cameron, on the other hand, is still standing in the doorway staring at me. I can't bring myself to look at him, I can only feel his eyes on me. I hear footsteps come ,then tingles under my chin as my face is tilted up to look at him. "Do you mean that?" He asks. "I mean everything I just said." I'm blushing, and Ace is still sitting in the chair across from

Cameron's desk, still laughing. Cameron leans down to my ear and says,

"This is not the place to have this conversation. But know that we will have it later." He kissed my ear and then slid in behind me on the sofa. Handing me my phone, I open it and proceed to check my messages. Surprisingly, I do have messages from Leah. She must have been informed that they gave her up as the source. Because the kind friend I once knew was completely gone. And here in my messages is a hateful and vengeful woman.

Leah: You fucking bitch! How could you have your fucking boyfriend end our contract. We are all going to lose our jobs because you are a fucking stuck-up prude. You won't win. They are coming for you. Your boyfriend might be rich, but he can't save you. They are going to ruin you, and I can't wait to watch you beg for your pathetic life.

I look up at Cameron after reading it out loud. He is fuming! I can feel the anger in the room. Between him and Ace, it's thick. I am crying because I was feeling safe, but after reading that message, the safety I once felt has completely crumbled. "So, Ace, do we have a plan in mind?" Cameron says roughly. "Yes, I do have a plan, but I am thinking that it's best if you are not involved in it. Let me take care of this part. I will touch base with you guys in a few days with an update." He then rises from his chair and walks towards the door. "Cameron, do you want me to post some men around? They can keep an eye out discretely." He reassures us. "Thank you Ace, that would be great." Cameron says. Before I know it, I am being carried out of his office and up stairs to his room. It must be pretty late by now. All the house staff are gone, and everything is dark. I felt Cameron hugged me tighter to him, and he whispered reassuring words in my ear. That's when I realized my entire body was shaking with fear. "Baby girl, I will not let anything happen to you. Please believe me. Ace is on it, and he and his men will protect you as well." I know he is trying to help, but I'm honestly just feeling too broken right now.

Chapter 13

ACE

I leave Cameron's house pissed off. I have seen my fair share of deranged people. But this girl is being hunted to be deflowered and ruined all for setting a boundary for her body that she wasn't ready to cross. How completely fucked up. I have seen this before, but it wasn't because of someone getting their ego hurt. Neither is okay, and I will forever live with the consequences of my previous actions. But I will not allow this girl to be harmed. I get to my bike and pull out my phone. It's 11:30 pm, but I know my guys will still be up. I ring my second in command. I tell him to send our two best out here to Cameron's house to discretely keep watch. I get a grunt of conformation. I then tell him to gather four others and wait for me at the clubhouse. It is about a half-hour to forty-five-minute drive to Cameron's, depending on traffic. I park my bike and head into the clubhouse. Once inside, I gather the four men waiting for me and we go straight to my office. I recap the situation with Layla, and as I thought, they all saw red. But before we do anything hasty, we must find a starting point. So, we searched the college and found out who the Dean is. He is our first target. Once searching for him and finding out all the essential information. We found he is divorced and lives alone, as his son, who is in his final year of college, lives on campus. So we take a drive.

CAMERON

Layla is a complete mess. I honestly have no idea how to help her right now. So I just carried her to our room. I set her on the bed and covered her with the blanket. She reaches for me, and I have to reassure her I will be right back. Running into the bathroom, I'm pretty sure that's the fastest I've ever used the restroom. Stripping to my boxers, I come back out into the room, and she is sitting up, hugging her knees, staring at me as I come back out. I go to the bed and climb in beside her. I pull her to me, and after a few moments, her full body shakes are gone. She keeps backing into me. I don't know if she is doing it for comfort or for heat. But either way, I'm officially turned on again, and it's pretty hard to hide when she keeps backing into it. She eventually turns till she is facing me. "Cameron, you are poking me." She says, but it's dark, and I can not tell if she is being playful or not. "I am sorry, baby girl. It's hard not to when you keep backing into me. But I am under control darlin; you have nothing to worry about." I say, reassuring her she is safe. "I don't want you to be in control, sweets." She says as she shoves me to my back and brings herself above me so she is straddling me. "Baby girl, I'm really trying here." I groan out. She isn't listening to me, though. She seems to not care that with every touch and roll of her hips against me I am losing my battle in strides. I have my head back with my eyes closed. Trying to enjoy her boldness but also trying to hold myself together. It's at that moment that I feel her tongue come across my right nipple. I freeze. God, that felt good, and that's new. But she is in her own world and doesn't even notice that I'm panting harder. She doesn't let up on my nipple; instead pulls the whole thing into her mouth, and I swear I am about to explode! "Darlin, I'm going to cum if you don't stop." I'm panty, and my voice comes out breathy. "You can touch me, you know." She says, completely ignoring what I just said to her. I mean, I do have a hold of the hips as she is grinding on me. But she clearly isn't satisfied with that. So I hook my finger into her sweats and pull them down far enough she kicks them off. I reach down, and my breath catches; she is dripping all over. I slide a finger inside her as she continues to assault my nipples. She gasps as my finger enters her, but she doesn't stop. Instead, she just rides my hand. "Good girl." I praise her. She brings her mouth to mine, and I melt. Losing all control I once had. I flip her over immediately. She gasped at the sudden change but never stopped her movement. She is a moaning mess. "Are you going to come for me, baby girl?" I whisper in her ear. "Fuck." she screams, and I can feel her convulsing around my finger. I damn near cum myself with all the sensations. I keep moving my hand to prolong her pleasure until she is done. I remove my hand, and she watches me lick it clean. I pull my length from my boxers and start to stroke, letting the tip smack her stomach as I go. She reaches down and stops me. I'm confused. "Stop jerking off and put your dick inside me." She says, biting my ear lobe and causing shivers to run down my spine. "Are you sure, Layla? With everything going on right now, you don't have to do this." Turning serious. But she wasn't having it. Layla grabbed me and lined me up with her entrance. "I love you, Cameron. And if you feel the same way, make love to me right now!" She looks unsteady when I don't move. I know I overheard her conversation with Ace earlier. But to hear her say it to me makes my heart ache with happiness. I lean down and smash my lips to her roughly and thrust into her all the way to the hilt. I felt her gasp as I broke her hymn. Once in, I stay still and wait. "Are you okay? How bad does it hurt?" I ask her, panicking because she isn't responding to me. I go to pull out, but she hisses and wraps her legs around me, holding me in place. "Baby girl, please talk to me." I plead. "You love me." She simply states. "Of course I do, Since the moment I met you. Now tell me about the pain, baby." I plead once again. "I'm okay sweets, really. Just move slowly till the sting stops." Groaning in the displeasure of having to move slow. Because now that I am in her, every carnal need is trying to force its way to the surface. But I do as she says. I start to hear her moaning and pick up my pace. God, she is so tight and wet, and I am barely hanging on. I've got a good pace going, and my baby is a hot mess. I reach between us and massage that sensitive spot. Within seconds, she is crumbling beneath me. But I am not done with her. I let her high die down a little. Then I lift her and give her a sweet, soft kiss. She returns it looking tired. "I'm not done with you yet baby girl." Her eyes widen. And I flip her to her stomach in one swift motion. Layla squeaks in surprise but arches her back for me. "Good girl" I praise her as I kiss from her ear down her neck and shoulder. I grab my shaft and slowly slide back into her. I feel her spasm around me, and she lets out a breathy moan. "Fuck Cameron. You feel so good, I am so glad I waited for you." She whispers. "You Better hang on, Darlin." I say, then I pull all the way out to just the tip and Slam back in. I expected her to whimper, but instead I received a "Fuck, Yes!" From her. So, by God I kept going. "Layla baby, I'm not going to last much longer. Do I need to pull out?" I asked hurriedly, "Oh sweets, you better fucking not." She says. So I don't; I go harder and harder; I finally hear her moaning out my name and start to spasm around me. I bury myself deep and let myself finally have the release I've been begging for for days.

LAYLA

Well, I did it. It was the most painful and pleasurable experience of my life. Oh, also Cameron loves me to. "That was amazing." I say to Cameron as he lays beside me, pulling me to him. "Baby girl, You have no idea!" He says, kissing my forehead. "Should we get cleaned up?" I ask him "I guess" he groans. Pulling me out of bed with him, we headed to the bathroom. "How sore are you?" he asks, concerned, lacing his features. "Well, I feel sore, but you carry me everywhere, so it's hard to tell." I laugh. He smiles and sits me on the counter. Going over to the bath, he gets the hot water running and adds different salts and oils than normal. "Why different oils?" curiosity getting the best of me. "These will help you heal faster. That's why I asked how sore you were. A bath with the right additives will help where taking a quick shower won't do much to help other than just get us clean." He explains. I don't think I will ever get used to how much he takes my well-being into consideration before he does anything. I wonder to myself if it will always be this way. "Are you always going to be this conscious of my well-being, or will that change once we get this whole situation resolved." I didn't mean to blurt that out, and I instantly covered my mouth. Luckily, he doesn't get offended. Just lifts my shirt off and smiles down at me. "Darlin, yes I have been tip-toeing here and there because of what is happening. But I do that because I care about your feelings and well-being, none of which will ever change. Now get naked so we can get cleaned up." He says, smirking at me. I finish undressing, and we get in the tub. After a couple more rounds in the tub, we finally managed to get cleaned up properly and get out. Finally settled in bed, I drifted off to sleep, snuggled into Cameron. Dreams of Roman and Leah plague my mind. They have captured me and have me tied down. Beating me and having their way with me. There is someone else there though; they stand in the background, and I can't see their face. Right as they start walking into the light, I am woken up by Cameron, who sounds panicked. "What, what's wrong?" I sit up wide awake now. That's when I noticed that his concerned face was staring at me. "Layla, you were screaming in your sleep, and you covered in sweat. Are you okay?" Oh, that is all that comes to mind. I flop back down on the bed and start to tell him about my dream. "Layla, darlin, you don't have to worry about that. I am *going to keep you safe." He sounds so serious. I half-heartedly smile at him. He looks hurt, and I know that he knows the truth. "You don't think I can keep you safe, do you?" He asks quietly. "I would like to believe that you can. It's just everything that Leah said in her message. It broke all safety I did feel. She seemed so serious and." I don't get to finish what I'm saying because Cameron climbs out of bed and starts pacing. "You gave yourself to me. Not because you love me but because you didn't want them to take it." He won't even look at me, and it stung that he was mostly right. I do love him, that part he is wrong about. "I do love you, Cameron! I never lied about my feelings for you. But yes, I wanted to experience my first time with you and find out how good it could be. Could you imagine if you couldn't protect me and they did get me. If they did have their way with me against my will. It's terrifying to think about especially if it was my first time. They would not show me the care and consideration that you did for the pain and soreness; they wouldn't care Cameron." I'm crying because I feel bad for not being completely honest with him about why I wanted last night to happen. "I'm sorry; I should have been completely honest with you last night. I thought that if I told you the whole truth, you wouldn't want me to do it. And it was what I needed and what I wanted!" I tell him. He is stopped now but still not looking at me. "I think I am more disappointed in the fact that you don't think I can keep you safe. Last night was amazing, no matter what your reasoning and I wouldn't take it back. But to know you don't feel safe with me is what hurts the most." Finally, he looks at me and I see it. The tears slid down his face. I did that. I put those tears there, and I feel like such a shit person right now. "Please don't cry. It's not your fault; you have done and are doing everything to keep me safe, and I appreciate everything you are doing for me. It's the seeds from Leah's message that planted doubt in my mind. And I'm sorry that I let it get to me so much. I do believe in you and in Ace. Please* don't be upset with me, Cameron, I'm trying over here. I've got a lot going on right now." I plead with him. He is still looking at me, but I see his face soften. He is still hurt but not as upset. "Layla, I understand. Your entire life has been completely flipped upside down and threatened. I am trying to be okay, but it's hard for me to. I want to keep you safe because I don't want to lose you, but I need you to be honest with me no matter what. From here on out, even if you don't think I will agree, I at least need you to be honest." He says, crawling back into bed. "I promise" I say, wiping away the few tears left on his face. Leaning in, he presses the softest of kisses on my lips before pulling me to him. We snuggle back in, and eventually, sleep takes me again.

CHAPTER 14

ACE

~

Too easy. We got to the Dean's house, and boy was that fun. For someone who acts so tough for the college. He was a crybaby bitch. He gave us all the information we needed on his son. We found out the lie that was said about our precious Layla to get her kicked out of school. That little bitch even gave us the whereabouts of his son. Turns out he is not a very good son and has been lying to dear old dad about living on campus. Seems daddy isn't too happy with his little boy. We wore masks and used voice changers to keep ourselves safe from our identities being seen. We left him tied up in a chair as we left and headed back to the clubhouse to regroup. Come morning, I will make my way back to

Cameron's house to give them the information we received. Before we go after pretty boy Johnny. "Get some shut-eye, boys. We reconvene back at the club 7 sharp." They all nod and head home. It's currently 2am, so I don't bother going home. I have a cot in my office, so I just head to my office and crash.

CAMERON

I wake up to hear my phone buzzing. I glance at the clock and see it's 7:15 am. Grabbing my phone, I saw Ace's name and picked it up immediately. "Anything?" I ask right away. "I will be there in an hour to fill you in." then he hung up. Looking over, I see Layla still asleep and latched on to my other arm like her life depended on it. And I guess it kind of does. I lay here remembering what happened last night when I woke her from her nightmare. I am still hurt, but I can understand why she is skeptical. I roll into her and pull her closer to me. She stirs a little. "We need to get up darlin." I whisper. She groans and snuggles deeper into me. I can't help but chuckle at her. She is so dang cute. "Ace will be here in an hour with an update." I say. That has her twisting to look up at me. "He has an update already?" She asks. "I told you, baby girl" he is the best. Now, let's get cleaned up and get around. I need to get to my office and check in with my secretary to make sure all is well at the office." "Oh my gosh, I am so sorry I pulling you from work. You missed yesterday and now today." She feels bad I can see guilt written all over her face. "Darlin, I can work from home. And honestly, the company can run without me. I have just never let myself relax enough to step away for a moment." I say. "Honestly, they are probably happy I am taking some time to myself. They are always harping on me for being the first one there and the last one to leave. My mother also. She wants me to settle down and let the company run itself. That is what we hired others to do, she always says. But I just got so used to not trusting people that it leaked into my work. But then I met you, and you made me want to trust people. You make me want to be with you all the time. But in thecase you are unemployed now, You can just come with me!" I say excitedly. "You want me to come to work with you? Won't I be in the way? I don't want to distract you." She says, worried, but there is something else, mischief, that's it. When she said she didn't want to distract me her eyes sparkled, and now I'm intrigued. "And how exactly would you be distracting me?" I ask, grinning ear to ear. "Oh, I don't know." She waves me off, and I see the spark dim. She is unsure of herself, and that makes me a bit sad. But I don't pray. "Alright, well let's go get cleaned up." I said, pulling her from the bed. After a quick shower, we get dried off, and I head into the walk-in closet. I get dressed in my business attire. She walks in wrapped in a towel, and she is so damn gorgeous. I instantly pull her to me and into a heated kiss. She responds immediately, but this is all we can have for now. Ace will be here soon. Slowly, I pull back from her, smile and kiss her nose. "Will you wear one of your new outfits today?" I ask. "Of course I will, sweets. If I'm going to the office with you, I can't really walk around looking homeless now, can I." she says, laughing. I just laugh at her because, honestly she could look homeless, and I would still think she was the most beautiful woman. She gets dressed and does her hair. Ace is walking into the house as we are descending the stairs. We all head straight to my home office. As soon as the door closes behind us. "Well, you aren't able to be deflowered anymore, now are you?" Ace says to Layla. "What!" Layla whisper yells. "You are carrying yourself differently. More confident, less afraid. This tells me that you are no longer as afraid of them because what they want from you is no longer available." He looks at me then, and I just nod his way. Layla is completely mortified. "I don't mean to offend you, Layla. You are your own person, and I'm sure losing it to Cameron here was a better experience then they would give you. It is actually better for us this way. Because now they are after something that no longer exists. It's easier to play them now." Ace is smiling at Layla. No judgment, all concern.

LAYLA

How the fuck did he just do that! He just called me out, and all I did was walk into a room before him. He isn't judging me, though he just looks concerned. "Layla, are you okay? With what's happening. No offense to you Cameron, none at all." Cameron looks confused by Ace's question. "Yes, Ace I'm okay. It was my decision. And Cameron took good care of me." I looked over at him to see him smiling at me. "Good, I'm glad. I am happy for both of you. Truly happy! Now, let's get to business." *Ace says. He fills us in on the information they got. Not how they got it, though. Which left me curious, but I know that he won't tell me no matter how much he seems to like me. He told us that they know where Johnny is staying and that is their next move. After our conversation was over, he stood and reached for my hand. I gave it to him after confirming with a glance to Cameron, who nodded. Ace pulled me to my feet and gave me a big bear hug. The kind you would get from a big brother. Holding me at arm's length, he says,* "Layla, I promise that I won't let anything happen to you. You have my word. You need me, you call." *He then walks to Cameron and gives him the same type of hug, only more of a side hug, you know, the way guys do it. He says something to Cameron, but I can't hear him. Cameron looks at me and smiles softly.* "I'll be in contact when I have more information." *Then Ace walked out. I stand there, confused by what has just happened.* "What was that about?" *I ask Cameron. Cameron walks toward me slowly. Pulling me into him, he whispers,* "He said that no matter what, he wouldn't let the past repeat itself." *I don't understand. And it must show on my face.* "Come Darlin, I will explain on the way to the office." *We grab a quick breakfast on our way out the door. Heading for one of his cars, he stops short.* "what do you want to take today?" *He asks me.* "I'm fine with one of the cars today." *I mean, I have been riding in the SUV the last couple of days, and it's nice, but it's also big. Nodding, we continued to walk toward the car. Like the gentleman he is, he opens my door and helps me in. He hopped in, and we were off to his office. We sit in silence for a few minutes, and then Cameron speaks.* "Ace had a little sister. I won't get into it because it isn't my story to tell. But let's say your situation has brought up a lot of bad memories for him. Because of some previous bad decisions, Ace lost his sister in one of the worst ways. And I think that is why he has become so attached and protective over you. He means no harm to you at all." *He was really vague. But I understand,*

I guess. He doesn't want to tell me in case Ace doesn't want me to know.

"Alright." Is the only thing I can think to say. I sit back, and we sink back into a comfortable silence for the rest of the drive to his office.

Chapter 15

ACE

I don't know why I feel this way. Layla she just draws me in. Not in a sexual way. But she feels like a cooling gel on a burn. She soothes something in me that I didn't know I needed. I hoped that Cameron didn't get offended, but I couldn't help but pull her close. I saw her quick glance his way for permission. He clearly gave it to her, or she wouldn't have given me her hand. Cameron knows more about me than anyone, not in my club. And I would trust him with my life same as I know he would with me. I think he understands he didn't growl at me this time. I smile to myself, remembering when I met Layla Just the day before, and he literally growled at me for staring at her. She is calming and pure. Even not being a virgin anymore, still pure. It's her soul that drew me in, not her body. She belongs with Cameron; he needs someone so pure and soothing. I'm still in my thoughts when I pull up to the clubhouse. Park my bike and throw the kickstand down all on autopilot. "Boss, when do you want to head out?" one of my guys pulls me back to the present. But I was startled by his presence because I didn't hear him walk up, and I automatically pulled my gun on him. His eyes go wide, but he doesn't make any moves. I shake it off, literally. I drop my gun and holster it. "Sorry brother, my mind was elsewhere, and I didn't hear you approach." I say sincerely. "Give me a minute I'll be right back." I walk off to my office and try to shake away the moments with Layla. Right now, I need to be the biker and club leader that I am. I freshen up quickly and head out to the conference room, where everyone is waiting for me. "Alright, guys we know where the little prick is that started all this. But we tread lightly and dress casually to not draw attention. Particularly because it's uncertain whether his father was able to escape and alert him. We scope from a safe distance until we are sure he is clueless about last night. We need to get him when he is least expecting it. Catch him off guard. We will split into teams of two. Myself and Chaz will take the first run to see what we are working with. If this kid is smart, he will be paying attention to his surroundings for new faces. So keep your distance. I want at least one other team of two at least a block away, and out of sight in case we need backup." I told them. "As long as everyone understands the plan, let's all head out and get changed into something less head-turning." I stood and made my way out. This kid is smart. We are a block away, and I can see the security cameras from here. The house he has been renting is secluded at the end of this road. Close enough to other houses to not look suspicious. But far enough away that he can see someone coming. This is going to be tricky. I call in one of our female members. She is a badass and not to be messed with. But I need her to do our recon because she is likely the only one who will be able to gain access. Lindsey shows up in low-rise bellbottom jeans and an off-the-shoulder crop top. I give her the details of this mission but warn her to be careful. We need her to pretend to be lost in hopes this creep is willing to help our girl out. I watch as Lindsey plays the part perfectly. She drives up to the curb and gets out. Turns in circles, looking at her surroundings and acting confused. She walks up to the house next door and knocks. Luck is in our favor, and no one answers. This is good because it shows she didn't go straight to his house. Johnny Boys house is next. Lindsey walks up, knocks on the door, and our boy answers in a few moments. He Gives Lindsey a predatory smile as he invites her in. We put a camera on her bracelet to give us a view of the inside. He is showing her around like the creep he is. She is sure to get a sweep of everything in view. Once given the directions she needs, Lindsey gives our creep a show-stopping smile a big thank you, and leaves his house. Luckily, she isn't who he is after otherwise, this could have gone differently. Lindsey gets in her car and drives backward to the previous road to turn, not giving this dickhead a picture of her license plate. Smart girl. As directed, she goes straight back to the clubhouse to safety in case this guy tries to pull anything. There isn't much we can do right now with all the surveillance. So we packed up and headed back to the clubhouse to go through the footage of the house and come up with a new plan.

LAYLA

I am super nervous as we pull into the underground parking garage at Cameron's head office. I started to feel self-conscious am I underdresser will I get in his way? What will people think of me just hanging out here with him? Probably that I am just desperate for his attention. Oh geez, my anxiety hasn't spiraled like this since the day I met Cameron. But as always, Cameron can see it on my face. We have parked now, and he is staring at me with a look of concern. "Are you okay darlin?" He asks, reaching to cup the side of my face. I lean into his hand and take a deep breath. Breathing him in for a moment, I respond. "Yes, just nervous. I don't feel like I belong here, and what people will think of me just sitting around your office all day." He smiles at me and pulls me onto his lap, so I'm straddling him. "Baby girl, you belong anywhere I am. And I don't care what these people think about you hanging around in my office all day. The only person I care about is right here." He leans in and kisses me softly. "Plus, with everything going on, I will not be inclined to remove you from my sites until it's resolved. And maybe not even after, I haven't decided yet."

He ends with a chuckle. I smile and lean down to rest my head on his shoulder. I breathe in all his scent, and it helps to calm me. He gives me a few moments to relax before he opens his door and sets me on the ground. "You ready Darlin?" He whispers. "Yes, let's go." I say as I grab his hand. Cameron interlocks our fingers and smiles down at my open show of affection between us. He gives me a goofy grin before he turns serious, and we head for the elevator. This elevator takes us to the lobby, and then we have to cross the lobby to another elevator that takes us straight to Cameron's floor. I can feel eyes on us the whole walk across the lobby. Some people have even stopped to stare, which I think is a little much. When I glance up at Cameron, he still has his serious face on and is looking straight ahead, not giving any of the on-lookers his attention. Once in the elevator and the doors close I breathe out a large breath I must have been holding. Cameron looks down at me and smiles. "Don't pay them any mind Darlin, no one has ever seen me with a girl before let alone one as gorgeous as you. People are bound to stare just try to ignore them as best you can." He says reassuringly. I just give him a small smile and nod. I don't like being the center of attention, and he is likely used to it. So it is easier said than done, but I'll give it my best shot. The doors open, and his serious face is back. With our fingers still laced, he pulls me out of the elevator, and I step into stride with him as we walk. There isn't a lot on this floor that I can see. It looks like a long hallway with a couple of offices, but they all look empty except for what I can assume is Cameron's. Stopping at the desk a few feet from his office, Cameron greets his receptionist and asks for anything he has missed while out. Her head was down this whole time working. When she finally looked up to respond to Cameron, she jumped. Like literally. Her eyes went from Cameron and back to me a few times before she got herself under control. "Sorry, Sir you startled me. I must have been hyper-focused." She stutters out. "It's fine Candy; we have been stared at all morning. *Layla, this is Candy; she is my receptionist. Candy, this is my girlfriend Layla. She will be hanging out with me in my office today. Layla, if you need anything when I am not in my office, please just get with Candy. She is a wonderful receptionist, and I'm sure she wouldn't mind some company here in there if you get bored of me."* He looked down and winked at me, and I just chuckled at his antics. *"It's lovely to meet you, Layla! And he is right; it does get kind of lonely on this floor. You are welcome to come hang out anytime!"* Candy looks genuinely excited to meet and hang out with me. *"Thank you, Candy it's nice to meet you too, and I would love that."* I say because, honestly, having no friends suck, and to be able to talk to someone, even if it isn't about anything personal, would just be a welcomed change. We proceed into

Cameron's office once Candy gives him his list of things he has missed while gone. Once in, he closed the door and pulled me into a hug. Kissing the top of my head, he says, *"My office is yours, baby girl. Get comfy; we are going to be here for a while.* I nod into his chest. Once he releases me and steps back, I take in his giant office. The back wall behind his desk is a floor-to-ceiling view of the city. He has two rather comfy-looking chairs in front of his desk and a long sectional that takes up a side corner of the office. He has a door off to the side of the couch that I open to reveal an entire bathroom suite, shower and all. I turned to him with a questioning gaze. He looks sheepish as he says, *"I told you I get to into my work. Which sometimes means I've slept on that sectional and showered here in the morning."* My eyes go wide, and He has literally done nothing but work since he took over from his dad. *"I'm sorry that life has come to that for you. I know it has been your decision to pour yourself so heavily into work. But you haven't been able to make time to live for yourself, sweets."* I say softly. He walks up to me and sweeps me up bridle style, and I squeak due to the suddenness. He sits on the couch with me and kisses me.

It's not light like earlier in the car. This is full of passion and longing, it's full of love. Breaking the kiss, he cupped my face between his hands. "I have never had a reason to live for myself. That is, not until I met you." He says with such conviction I feel tears well up in my eyes. I plead with them not to fall, but they don't like me because they come streaming down anyway. Smiling down at me, Cameron wipes my tears, kisses my forehead and then shifts me to the couch so he can stand. "I need to get some work done." As he strides over to his desk, a knock sounds at the door. I sit up straight right as Cameron tells the person to come in. "Sir, sorry for the intrusion. The new laptop you asked for just came in." Candy walks to give Cameron the new laptop. Stopping in front of his desk, he stops her. "Thank you, Candy, but that Laptop is for Layla." He says casually. "What?" I say, bewildered by what he just said. "Yes,

Darlin, I had a new laptop brought in so that you could start searching for online schools to start getting back into your original plan of what you want to do." I'm just staring at Cameron; he paused but then continued.

"Layla, you didn't get to finish your schooling, and it wasn't because you are not smart or you didn't show up. It was because of some punk kid and his inflated ego. So, yes, I bought you a laptop so that you could at least try to get back into the architecture program and get started again. Even if it's only from the online classes until we can figure things out." My insides are in full battle mode. I am melting on one side that he was thoughtful enough to do this for me. But I am also pissed because he knows I don't have the money for this right now, and he is going to pay for it whether I like it or not. "Cameron, you know, with everything that has happened, I don't have the extra money right now to pay to get back into school. I appreciate the thought, really I do. But I will not let you pay for this, so don't even

think about it!" I end that by giving him a raised eyebrow, daring him to do it anyway. Instead, he shocked both Candy and me as he busted out laughing. "What on earth is so dang funny?" I ask him, confused. Candy looks shell-shocked. She looked between the two of us like she had never seen this side of Cameron before. But she seems so confused about what to do with the laptop that she just continues to stand there. "I'm laughing darlin, because you think you have a choice today." I give him my hardest look. But I think it's having the opposite effect. "Oh goodness, you are cute when you are mad. But seriously Layla, having your degree is important. And I know it's something you are passionate about. Just do me a favor and just look some up. We can handle everything else later." He says it calmly, but his eyes are pleading with me. Candy must see it too because she walks over to me and sets the laptop on the coffee table. She gave me a big smile and a wink before she turned and walked back out of the office.

Chapter 16

CAMERON

I knew Layla was going to fight me on paying for her to go back to school and finish her degree. I expected nothing less from her. What shocked me was that she did it in front of Candy my receptionist. It's not a big deal, and

I could careless. But Layla had been so concerned all morning about what everyone was going to think of her today at the office, and the first thing she did with no hesitation was call me out. God, I loved it. Candy was completely speechless and didn't know what to do. Because even though I have never been rude or disrespectful to anybody here, people don't talk to me like that. At least not in the eyes of the people that work for me. If Candy hadn't been in here, I would have pulled my girl into the bathroom so we could have settled it on the counter. I know my baby girl was mad and trying to let me know. But it was probably one of the hottest things I've ever seen. And I just wanted to bend her over and fuck that attitude right out of her. But instead, I pleaded with her for a compromise until we could come to a mutual ground on the situation. Without giving her time to argue, Candy walked over and set the laptop on the table in front of Layla. I don't know what kind of look Candy gave her. But it's got my girl blushing. I smile to myself because I can't get enough of the way she looks wearing that blush. But I don't tease her about it I just sit down and get to work. After a few moments, I glance over to see that Layla has opened the new laptop, and it looks like she is deep in concentration. I hope she does as I have asked and at least looks into it. She deserves to finish her degree.

ACE

My men and I have been going over the video footage from Lindsey's bracelet cam. We were also able to get ahold of the blueprints to the house, showing the layout inside and out. This is going to be tricky, but it must be done. Our Tech guy was able to infiltrate the camera feed, and we could watch the feed up to a week's worth of footage, which was severely helpful. We have footage of a woman and guy coming and going a few times in the last week. We have taken screenshot images that I am going to print and take to Cameron's later this evening to see if Layla can recognize them. We are still trying to figure out how to get our hands on this Johnny kid. However being able to access his cameras will be helpful in keeping an eye on not only him but his schedule of comings and goings. We will need to get something done soon, though, or we risk his father telling dear old Johnny about what happened to him.

LAYLA

After the laptop incident this morning, everything has gone pretty smoothly. I decided to look at some online schools. I must have been really focused because I didn't hear Cameron get up from his desk and come over to me. Lifting me quickly and setting me back down on his lap, I gasped and almost yelled in surprise. I look up to see him grinning that same goofy grin from earlier. Even though I'm still upset with him for bombarding me with the laptop this morning. I can't help but relax and melt into him. He brings his chin down to rest on *my shoulder. "Have you seen any that you like?" He whispers into my ear. "I don't know. It's been over three years since I've had to look into these types of things, and I'm feeling a little overwhelmed by all the options." I say back. "It's okay baby girl, and you have time. I just want you to be happy. You don't have to choose or make anything permanent today. I just figured being here all day would get boring, and if we are going to make it a habit. Being able to go back to school, even if it's only online for now, is something you could do while you are here with me." He says lightly. He knows I'm still upset, and he is trying to rationally reason with me. And that is even more frustrating because he is right. If I'm not working I am going to be here all day doing nothing. It would make sense that I can go back to school and be productive. I groan in frustration, and I hear him sigh behind me. I lean forward, setting the laptop on the table. I turn and straddle his lap. He looks like a puppy that got kicked. Pressing my forehead to his, I know without a shadow of a doubt that I'm going to give him whatever he wants. I'm still going to give him a hard time and not make it easy for him, but eventually, I'm going to give in. I take a deep breath and kiss him softly. Cameron moans into my mouth, turning the kisses heated. I feel his hard cock pulse in front of my core, and without thought, I start to grind on him. Cameron picks me up without letting up on our kiss, and when he finally breaks away, I realize we are in the bathroom. He turns and closes the door, locking it. He looks at his watch and says. "We have to make this quick, love. I have a meeting soon." Without hesitation, I start stripping my clothes. Cameron does the same. Once done, he pulls me to him, and our heated make-out begins again. I feel Cameron's hands grab the back of my thighs, and I'm being lifted. Once high enough, I wrap my legs around him. He repositions his hands to my ass and shifts me closer to him. He backs me to a wall, and I slowly ease down onto his cock. My breathing is fast and wanting as he takes his time to build up the pressure within. I can feel his heavy breathing on my neck as he kisses and nips at my jaw and collarbone. I feel hot and needy as I whine for a faster pace. He makes eye contact with me, grinning big he slides all the way out to the tip before thrusting all the way back in deep. I moan out at the pleasure, though it isn't enough. I try to move to get him to move, but he stays where he is. I groan and open my eyes to look at him. He looks serious as he says, I hope you can handle what you are asking for. My eyes widen, but I nod with determination. He smiles and adjusts his hands on my ass for a better grip. Then all I know is Cameron. Everything else has completely faded away. It's pain mixed with pleasure, and I can't get enough. I'm a moaning mess, my head resting back against the wall as Cameron fucks me hard and thoroughly in his office bathroom. The pressure within me is almost at peak height. "Open your eyes, baby girl. Let me see how you look when I fill you with cum." Cameron says, his voice is rough and sexy, and I know he is almost there too. I keep eye contact with him as I fall to pieces on his cock. His full body shudders as he takes me in and then reaches his own orgasm, hard and rough, with two last merciless thrusts all the way to the hilt. After, shocks pulse through me as he continues to thrust slowly to prolong my pleasure. Finally, he slowly pulled out and just hugged me. Pressed up against this wall and secured in place by Cameron. I feel free, like everything in my life isn't happening, and I am free to go out and finish my degree with no worries, like everything is okay. Cameron kisses my forehead, turns, and sets me on the counter. Grabbing a warm wash rag, he cleans me up and then himself. We get dressed in a comfortable silence. Once we left the cover of the bathroom, I started to walk back to the couch. Cameron grabs my wrist lightly and pulls me to sit on his lap at his desk. Apparently, his meeting is virtual, and he turns his webcam off, so it's only audio. My legs drape across his lap, and I settle into his chest just resting my head on his heart. Cameron Kisses the* top of my head and begins his meeting. I find myself drifting into sleep, feeling the vibration of his voice through his chest. I wake to being lifted off of Cameron, and I panic and latch back on to him. I hear a deep chuckle from behind me and relax into Ace's arms.

Cameron looks at me to make sure I'm okay with Ace taking me from him, and I give him a small smile and nod. He nods and continues to work. I don't know what time it is, but it's dark outside those huge windows. Ace carries me to the couch. He grabs the throw blanket from the back and wraps me in it before sitting down beside me.

Chapter 17

ACE

I called Cameron to stop by his house with the pictures for Layla to look at. But when he answered, he said they were still at the office. I don't usually go to his office, but we are kind of on a time-sensitive mission. I head through the lobby and straight to the elevator that goes to Cameron's floor. There are only a handful of people still here, considering it's after 5 pm, so I don't have too many on-lookers as I make my way through. Once I reach his office, I knock and wait for him to tell me to come in. I strain to hear him as he is talking quietly. Once I enter the office, I see why. Layla is draped over him in his chair, peacefully sleeping. He gives me a sheepish grin, which makes me think it's his fault that she is draped over him. He really does love her. Can't even be across the room for a full work day. I grin at him but just shake my head as I walk over. "I need to borrow her." I say quietly. "You have more information?" Cameron asks. "Kind of; we were able to find that kid's house, but there were cameras surrounding it, so we had to improvise to get a look on the inside. We are forming a plan on how to grab him. We were able to hack into his camera's system, I've got pictures of a couple of people coming and going over the last week or so that aren't our prime target. I'm hoping to see if Layla can identify them for me." I say, still whispering like children. "Alright, but anytime I move, she wraps tighter, so you may have to take her from me." He says, looking upset at his own statement. I smile big at him, and he just shakes his head at me. He slides his chair back so I can pick Layla up. Once I start to slowly move her from his lap, her eyes pop open, panicked, and she latches back onto Cameron. I chuckle because he definitely wasn't wrong about her wrapping tight. However once she hears my laugh, she must recognize me because she lets go of Cameron and allows me to carry her over to the couch. I didn't miss her and Cameron's silent exchange before I walked off with her. I can feel Cameron's eyes on me as I grab the throw from the back of the couch and wrap her in it like Cameron did the other night. I don't really know what compelled me to do that. I sit down beside Layla and give her a few moments to wake up a bit. "What time is it?" She asks. "around 5:30." I say to her. Her eyes widened. "I've been asleep for 4 hours?" She turned to look at Cameron, who just shrugged and went back to work. I laugh again at his lack of care attitude with her. I have always known him to have a strict schedule and be uptight about everything. But with Layla, he is relaxed and calm, like as long as she is there, it makes no difference when things get done as long as they get done. I make a mental note of the fact that she was draped over him and asleep on his chest for four hours, and he just continued to work like she wasn't there. "Do you feel okay enough to look at some photos for me?" I ask gently. Whoa, where did that come from. I glance up at Cameron, and his eyes are wide. He must want to know also. Layla doesn't even question it just nods her head. "I have surveillance photos of two people who have been hanging out with Johnny the last week or so. I just need you to look at the photos and tell me if you recognize them. Are you up for that?" My voice is still gentle, and I'm not sure what's going on. She nods again, so I grab the photos out of my pocket. As soon as I hand them to her, she gasps and starts to cry. "I didn't want to believe that you guys were right. I didn't want to believe that all this started three years ago. But it had to have been from that because that is Leah, and the other is Roman." She sobs. I pick her up and cradle her in my arms. What is it with this girl. I can feel Cameron's eyes on me. But I can't meet his eyes because I don't know why I feel this way either. I feel myself slowly rocking like you would soothing a child. It hits me, and for the first time in years, I'm crying. I feel Layla look at me; she isn't crying anymore and has calmed down. Twisting in my lap so she is sitting upright. Concern laces her features. "Why are you crying, Ace?" She asks it so gently and low that I break completely. I have no idea what just happened. I have gone years without crying over my sister, and now everything just seems so real, and Layla's soul is just so soothing to me like my sisters used to be. Before I knew what's happening, Layla was straddling me, not in a sexual way but to give herself access to me. She leans into me and gives me such a tight hug like she is trying to put all my broken pieces back together with this one hug. I hear Cameron join us on the couch. I can't meet his eyes. I feel too broken right now to deal with jealousy. But when I risk a glance, all I see is concern. Layla brings my attention back to her. "Talk to me Ace; what's happening?" She asks. "I'm okay; this situation just hits home, hard for me. But I'll be okay. The situation is about you and keeping you safe from all these assholes." I whisper to her. I know that Cameron can hear me; I'm not trying to hide from him. There isn't anything to hide; he knows about my past. I pick Layla up and set her on the couch because her being this close makes me want to continue this breakdown and spill all my emotional turmoil. But it's not her problem. She has plenty of her own right now. I stand, pull myself together, and go to walk out of the office. I'm halfway to the elevator when Cameron's hand grabs my shoulder. I turn to him, knowing he won't let this go. "Don't worry Cam, I will get this job done and make her safe again." I say. "I think I'm more concerned about you at the moment, Ace. What happened?" He is worried it's written all over his face. I take a deep breath and blow it out. How do I explain to him that I want to be around his girlfriend because she makes me feel at home? She reminds me so much of my sister. "She makes me feel whole again. Not in a sexual way, but she soothes the pain I feel. She just reminds me of my sister so much, and watching her fall apart broke me." I say quietly. "I understand the feeling; Layla eases the pain I normally feel for my dad and brother. There is no shame in wanting to stop hurting, to want to feel whole again. Ace, Layla trusts you to take care of her and protect her. I gave her my word you would, but she believes in you on her own now, not just because I told her she could." Cameron says. There is no judgment or jealousy. He strictly understands how I feel. "It's just a weird feeling to want to be around someone constantly that isn't blood-related and not in an attractive way. Don't get me wrong, man your girl is gorgeous. But it's like I just want to have the soul connection and nothing else." I say, bewildered that I even said that out loud. "Well, I don't remember Layla ever stating that she had siblings, so I guess you could adopt her as a sister. Then maybe you would feel so weird about wanting to be around her." Cameron suggests. I am considering it because it could work. It makes me not feel so weird about it if I just want to hang out with her like a brother. "I would like that. But it's something I would want her opinion on first." I say. Cameron nods and leads me back into his office, where Layla sits on the couch with her laptop.

LAYLA

I pull up my previous searches for colleges, trying to focus. But I just can't. My mind is whirling with everything going on. The fact that Leah and Roman somehow know Johnny. The fact that not sleeping with him has caused a three-year-long plot to destroy me! Then there is Ace. I feel connected to him, and watching him fall apart because I was falling apart was hard. I tried to hug him tight to show that I cared that he was okay. And I remember what Cameron had told me about Ace's sister. I can only assume it has to do with her and whatever happened to her. I could tell that he was embarrassed after he realized what he was doing and panicked, trying to leave. But everyone deserves to have a breakdown every now and then to want to be okay. I'm pulled from my thoughts when I hear the door to the office open. Cameron and Ace walk back in and stand in front of me. "Layla, I have something I want to talk to you about." Ace says. But he looks really nervous, so I try to put on a kind face to show him it's okay. Taking a deep breath, he just explodes with thoughts. "Layla, this is odd for me because I don't usually have this kind of attachment to people. But I really like spending time with you. You ease my pain, and it makes me feel almost whole again. I know that sounds kind of weird. I don't want anything from you other than to be your friend and spend time with you. Maybe like a brother? I promise I won't ever let anything happen to you, and I will protect you always!" He stutters. I sit there stunned by everything; he just rushes out when I hear Cameron speak. "Baby girl, you remember what I told you?" I nod. "Ace has been left with hurt and pain, same as myself and you. But something in you reminds him of his sister and it soothes the pain he feels. So he enjoys being around you like he enjoyed being around her." Cameron says. Ace looks confused, and I wipe a tear that slides down my cheek. "Cameron, you told her?" Ace looks angry. I get up and walk to Ace. I wrap my arms around his waist and hug him. He melts into me, and I say, "He told me nothing of what happened. Only that you had a sister and that something happened to her. But you vowed not to let the past repeat itself." I say lightly, hoping to ease his mind of Cameron's betrayal. Hugging me back, he sighed in defeat and said, "I guess that's only fair." He steps back and looks down at me. "My sister was a wonderful person. She cared about everybody, and I miss her a lot. I made one mistake, and it cost me her. I have not and will never put myself or my friends in that kind of position again."

He looks raw, and it's weird to see this badass club leader looking at me like this. But I already trust him to protect me. "Ace, you don't have to only come around for information. You are welcome whenever." I say to him. He lets out a breath I don't think he realized he was holding. He picked me up and whirled me around a few times before putting me down. "I'm sorry this got really mushy, guys. That wasn't my intention when coming here. But with that out of the way and me feeling better about things. I have a fuck boy to hunt down." He gives us a wicked grin and walks out.

CAMERON

I have never seen Ace so broken in all the years I have known him. That was excruciating to watch. I was a little leary of the way he was with Layla, not in a bad way. He was just being gentle, doing things he laughed at me for just a couple of days ago. I've never seen that side of him before. But after talking with him and getting the truth. I completely understand how he feels. I mean, I have that same connection with Layla, though ours is both attraction and a soul-bound connection. But I see wear she helps him and how he needs her in his own way. Layla, on the other hand, didn't even hesitate to give him a sisterly hug and be there for him. I'm lucky to have her! I'm sure she is feeling uneasy after finding out these people have been plotting against her for three years. I pick her up and sit on the couch for a bit in silence. "How are you holding up darlin?" I ask her. She just shrugs and leans into me. "I don't feel important enough to be someone's cause of three years worth of vengeance." She sighs. "But it is clear now that if they have waited this long. They don't plan on stopping." She smiles up at me. Her eyes are wrinkling with mischief. "But I know a guy who is going to teach them a lesson." She laughs. Thinking about the wicked look we got from Ace before he headed out.

Chapter 18

LAYLA

Finally, back to Cameron's house! Even after sleeping for 4 hours, I feel exhausted. As soon as we get inside, Mrs. Magnolia was there. Asking how things went at the office and if we had any issues. We filled her in on everything we know so far from Ace. Letting her know our day went fine at the office, with no major issues. By the time we got home, it was 7:30 pm; we just stopped on our way home and grabbed food. Cameron and I sit in the living room and talk with his mother for a little while before we all decide that we should head to bed. As usual, I don't get to walk. I have Cameron as my own personal carrier. Even if I wanted to walk, I don't think he would let me. Smiling to myself, I just wrapped my arms around his neck and let him carry me to his room. We walked in, and Cameron took me straight to the bathroom. Setting me on the counter, he started to undress to get into the shower. Once he starts the shower and sets the temperature, he comes back and starts taking my clothes off, too. Once we are both naked, he lifts me again and walks us into the cascading water. Leaning my head back, I just take in the heat of the water. Let it cleanse my mind. Cameron must sense that I am tired because he doesn't try to make anything sexual. He sets me down and puts shampoo in his hands, and starts to massage it through my hair and into my scalp. I still don't know how to get used to this. Grabbing my loofah, he adds body wash and gently scrubs the soap all over my body until he is satisfied that I'm clean. Once I'm rinsed, he does my hair all over again with conditioner. After I'm done, I do all the same for him. Showing my appreciation for what he does for me. Turning the water off, Cameron reaches for the towels; he wraps one around his waist, and the other he wraps around me before picking me up again and carrying me to the bed. I assume he isn't finished, so I just sit there waiting. I was right; he walked out of the walk-in closet, in a pair of boxers and carrying one of his shirts and a pair of my panties. He dries me and helps me put on his shirt and the panties he picked. Crawling into bed, he pulls me to him, and we rest comfortably. We haven't spoken since we came upstairs. It's a peaceful silence though, like an understanding of where we are together and how we are both feeling in this moment. Finally, words are spoken. I hear Cameron whisper, "I love you, baby girl" into my ear. I don't respond though; all I can do is feel myself drifting off to sleep, feeling loved and safe.

ACE

Man, I thought this punk was smart. Turns out it must be someone on his team. This kid is an arrogant prick who thinks himself untouchable. We stopped his cameras from working around the house. Sneaking in from the side opposite his neighbor, we were able to walk right in. He left all the doors unlock. We quietly searched the house, looking for anything that might help us. Eventually, we stumbled upon the exact person we came here for. Johnny is fast asleep in a recliner. Well, this was anti-climatic. Shoving a bag over his head, we rope him together and carry him out. That was way easier than I thought. Almost too easy. We throw the punk in the trunk of the car and take off to an abandoned building we set up just for this. Leaving the bag on, we get him tied to a chair. Once situated, we removed the bag from his face. To my surprise, this frat boy was crying. "What you crying for punk? We haven't even started." I ask abruptly. "Whatever you want, man it's yours. I didn't do anything." He stutters out. My men and I laugh at his attempt to plead with us. "I don't want your stuff punk. I want to know why you have been stalking and plotting against a girl for the last 3 years?" I don't feel like bantering with this pussy. I'm getting straight to the point, so we can be done here. Johnny's eyes widen. Good he should be afraid. "Come on, man we can work this out." He begs. "Can we though, because you have endangered someone I care about. And I am pretty sure you are going to have to pay for that." I give him a menacing smiling. Intern this kid pisses his pants. My smile turns to disgust as the smell of urine takes up the room we are in. "I swear I didn't have anything to do with some chick." Wow, lying straight to my face. "No? So you aren't the punk that got his feelings hurt when she told you she wouldn't sleep with you, and so you then proceeded to get her kicked out college?" I'm yelling, and Johnny is visibly flinching at every word I spit at him. "Yeah, I got upset she didn't sleep with me and did some irrational shit. But I haven't had anything to do with her since then." He looks exhausted, and we haven't even been here a full hour. "I don't believe you." I state calmly. "Why would I spend so much of my college life being worried about one girl. I have a pick from several girls who are more than willing to sleep with me." He says, putting his punk face back on. "Okay, so what about the other people you hang around?" I question. He seems unconcerned but confused. "What about the people I hang around? They don't even know her; that was three years ago." The nonchalant tone he says it with pisses me off. Not because he doesn't seem to care. But because he actually believes it. Fuck! "Can I tell you something Johnny." I ask him menacingly again. His face falls, but he nods. "Those friends of yours seem to be using you." I whisper. Shaking his head, he says, "They wouldn't do that." I sigh "Well, I hate to break it to you, kid. But Roman and Leah, they aren't your friends. They are using you to get to Layla. Putting you in the spotlight takes it off of them." I tell him. "Why would they do that. They don't even know her. They have only ever heard me talk about what happened." He says. "Well, they took it upon themselves to right the wrong that was apparently done to you, I guess. Your friend Leah made it a mission to work at the same place and become best friends with Layla. They even set up Roman to date her for a month. And when Roman tried to Rape Layla in her sleep and failed. They took their mission to higher lengths." His eyes are wide at my words. I don't like this punk-ass kid, but I can tell he had no idea what was happening. "I swear, man I had nothing to do with any of that. I might be a shit son and make irrational decisions sometimes. But I'm not a rapist, man." Crying again pathetic. "Here is what we're going to do, kid. You're going to help us catch them before they try to inflict more harm of any kind on Layla. And then after that, you are going to fix your fuck up of getting her kicked out of college so she can complete the degree she drove across the country to get." He looks hesitant. "You have a problem with that?" I ask. "What if they find out I know, and they try to hurt me too." The concern in his eyes is bullshit, but considering this kid only thinks of himself, I am not surprised. "Let's just say, if you don't. Your fate ends with us, the same as theirs." I glare down at him, and terror takes over his concern. Good.

Chapter 19

CAMERON

~

Waking up with Layla in my arms will never fail to be my favorite thing. I snuggle her closer, pulling her warmth into me. She stirs a little, and I pause. Waiting a moment to make sure she is still asleep. After a few moments, I crawl out of bed and get up to use the restroom. When I come back into the bedroom, Layla is awake. But still laying in bed watching me with a sleepy smile. I walk over and crawl back in beside her. Cuddling her to me again, I press my lips to hers softly. She instantly melts into me, and I love the feeling of it. The skin-on-skin contact is causing all the tingles we share to go straight to my dick. I can already feel it hard, tapping her stomach with each movement. She is grinding into me, and I know what she wants. She is only dressed in my shirt and a pair of panties. I pull her closer to me. Letting my dick free, she reaches down and grabs it. Stroking me lazily from the base all the way to the tip. I groan at the pleasure she's brought me. She leans up and starts kissing my chest all the way up to my neck and jawline. She pushes me slightly, so I roll onto my back, giving her access to be on top and do what she wants. She takes her time exploring me, kissing and nipping her way down. But she doesn't put her mouth on my dick like I thought she would. Instead, she stands, turns, and sits back down. I am now in full view of her back and ass. I reach out and grab a handful of it. She squeaks in surprise but doesn't move away. Instead, she moves her panties to the side and slides herself slowly down onto my cock. God, that was sexy as hell. I almost came just watching, let alone the feeling. I've never had someone ride me cowgirl style, and it feels amazing, though she is going slow, and it's agony. It feels so good, but I just want to grab her hips and thrust deep over and over again. She tilts back and puts her hands on my chest to sturdy herself as she searches for the right angle. "What do you need, baby girl?" I ask her. "I've got the spot, but I can't get enough friction and speed to get there." She is breathless, and her eyes hooded when she looks back at me. "Say no more." I groan, grabbing her hips just like I wanted, I move her to my rhythm. She must agree that's what we needed because she seems to be writhing in pleasure. She leans so far back, just letting me take control, that she is on her elbows now. Her back is almost touching my stomach, and her head rests on my chest. It's only a matter of seconds before she is screaming my name and making a mess of me and the bed. "Look at me, baby girl." Her eyes open, and she looks back my way. Pounding into her hard like my life depends on it. I cum hard, locking my mouth on her and rolling her into a second orgasm. "Fuck, the was amazing!" Layla says. "Oh, you thought I was done with you huh?" She raises an eyebrow at me before raising up and turns to straddle me the normal way. "Oh, there's more, is there?" She is trying to be coy. I take my finger and flick her still-swollen bud and she moans. Then looks down at me in shock. Before she can recover, I flip us, so she is under me now. "Are you ready Darlin?" I whisper into her ear. "Yes" she pants. But it was just above a whisper, and her eyes were hooded again. I drive into her hard and deep. I expect a wince because I'm trying to gauge how far I can go. Where her boundaries of pleasure and pain begin and end. But instead, I hear her breath out a "Fuck, yes." And that's the only thing I needed to hear. Grabbing where her thighs crease at her hips, I wrench her down, and I glide back in. She is so fucking wet that it's easy to slam in and out of her. No hint of pain; all I hear from her are *moans and heavy breathing. I reach down with one hand and flick her bud again, and she comes completely undone beneath me. I lean forward, putting my hands on the bed just above her shoulders to use as a stopper. Putting my mouth to her ear, I suck the lobe into my mouth and nip it. She groans out some more pleased sounds. "Hold on darlin it's going to get a little wild." Her eyes meet mine with a challenging smile. And I broke all resolve I had left to try not to go too rough. But she wants it, so I am going to give it to her. I rock back so till the tip slides out but doesn't leave the comfort of her nether lips. Slamming back in all the way to the hilt. I Slam my lips to hers, ravenous to taste her. She does as she is told and grabs hold of me as I keep pounding into her at an alarming pace. After a few moments, I feel her tighten around me, but I swallow her scream in my mouth as I pump one last time. I bury myself as deep as I can as I cum hard inside her. I hold for a few moments, both of us coming down from our highs. Then I slowly slide out of her. She whimpers at the loose, and I just kiss her forehead before standing. I pick her up and carry her to the bathroom, where I get a hot bath running for her. I put in all the proper salts and oils for her to relax in. I finish undressing her, pick her up, and set her into the tub. Leaning her head against the back, she looks up at me. "Are you not getting in with me?" She asks. "Not this time, baby girl. You need time to relax, and I am going to take a quick shower. Once I am done, I will come over and take care of you. But for now, relax and let the salts and oils help your muscles. She smiles, but it's lazy, like she could go back to sleep. I give her a soft kiss and walk over to the shower.*

LAYLA

Once done in the shower, Cameron does exactly as he says. Wrapping his towel around himself, he kneeled next to the tub and washed my hair and my body. Letting me lie and relax as he took care of me. Once washed, he helped me out and wrapped a towel around me. We go into the bedroom and get dressed. Heading downstairs we run into Mrs. Magnolia. Smiling up at me, she waves. Once I reach the bottom, she pulls me into a crushing hug. Which I accept wholeheartedly and return with enthusiasm. We all sit down and eat breakfast together. We were finishing up, and I was walking to put my dishes in the sink when someone grabbed me from behind. I scream, and a dark chuckle reminds me of my safety. "Dang it Ace! You scared the shit out of me!" I say, panic still lacing my tone. He sets me down, and I whirl around to face him. He doesn't seem too concerned with it as he tries not to laugh again. Reaching down, he picks me up again and twirls me around until I'm laughing and forgets all about why I'm mad. "Are you here to see Layla, or do you have something you need to share with us?" Cameron asks, walking up to us. "Both," Is all he says before he puts me down and drapes his arm over my shoulders. Ace walks us to Cameron's home office. Once we are all in the office, including Mrs. Magnolia, Ace starts. "Well, things went smoother than we thought. We were able to get to Johnny. Unfortunately, he had no idea what was happening to you." He says, squeezing me close. "Are you sure? He could be lying." Mrs. Magnolia cuts in. "No ma'am, I went at him pretty hard. When I brought up Leah and Roman, he was defensive. Saying they wouldn't do such a thing. They didn't even know Layla." Ace says. "So, if they weren't friends when everything happened three years ago. Then why would they come after me now?" I ask, completely confused. "According to Johnny, he has only ever talked to them about what happened. But they weren't friends back then. So, it seems as though they have taken it upon themselves to enact revenge on you for his sake. However, I believe he had no idea. The poor punk pissed himself and cried during our interrogation. I don't think he would have the stomach for the shit these two are pulling." Ace says, and I literally laughed out loud. I hurried and covered my mouth. But for someone who acted so tough three years ago. And now cried and peed his pants just to be interrogated wow. "Sorry, that was uncalled for." I apologize. And then everyone in the room erupts into laughter. "Baby girl, don't apologize. He had that coming to him." Cameron says between fits of laughter. "Either way, we now have a plan to catch them, and good Ole Johnny boy is going to help us. And once he is done helping us, he is going to fix everything with the College so you can go back and finish your degree." Ace says to me. "How. How did you convince him to do that?" I asked. He just smirked and gave me a look that said, "If I told you, I'd have to kill you." I just shake my head at him. "Let's get to it." Ace says, and he fills us in on the plan.

Chapter 20

LAYLA

Ace asked if he could hang out with me for the day. Therefore, I did not have to sit at the office all day while Cameron worked. I was fine to go and hang out. Cameron was a little reluctant to be away from me, but in the end, he agreed. "Alright, Layla. Have you ever ridden a bike before?" Ace asks as he hands me a helmet. "No." I state, trying to figure out how this helmet works. Turning to me, Ace helps me get it settled on my head the correct way, and then latches it under my chin. Tightening it to fit me snugly. He settles both feet on the ground and straightens. "Alright Layla, use my shoulders to steady yourself, then step on that peg and swing your leg over to the other side." Ace walks me through what to do. Once I get the courage to actually try it, I feel dumb. It was way easier than I thought it would be. I wiggle a bit to get comfy. "Wrap your arms around my waist and hold on tight, okay." Ace gives me more directions. He gave me a moment to do as I was told, and then the bike rumbled to life . I squeeze him tighter and feel his belly ripple in laughter before he takes off out of Cameron's driveway. We drive through town, heading to Ace's clubhouse. Passing several little shops I've never seen before. I lean forward. "Ace, can we stop and look at those shops? I don't ever remember seeing them before!" I shout over the roar of the motorcycle. He nods and pulls off on a side street to loop around. Ace backs us into a parking spot and cuts the engine. He stills and straightens, giving me his hand to help me get off the bike. Once I'm down, Ace flips out the kickstand, letting it rest on that as he climbs off. He helps me with my helmet. Putting my helmet and his leather jacket into the side bag. That's so weird, and I know that Ace is a big guy and can be intimidating. But without his leathers, he looks almost normal. Huh. "What?" He asks. "I was just thinking that without your leathers on, you look almost normal." I say, laughing lightly. He pulls me into his side, but I can feel his chuckle. After a bit, he let's go of me, and we started walking toward the shops I wanted to look at. We are on the third store when my stomach gurgles loudly. Ace grins "I think it's lunchtime." There is an outdoor Café around the corner. We walk around and have a seat at one of the tables. A little blonde girl walks up to take our order. She seems really nice, and when she asks what she can get us, Ace makes it known to her that I am his sister and not his girlfriend. Oh my, he likes her. I keep my grin hidden behind my menu. We order our drinks, and she saunters off. But not before turning and giving him a wink. He blushes, and I can't stop the oh my gosh face that shows. He glances my way. "Oh shut it, Layla!" He says shyly. I stifle a laugh and look back at the menu to see what I want to eat. "Hey, I'm going to go to the restroom. I'll be right back." Ace says. I can see the restrooms from where I'm sitting, so I nod, and he walks off. I'm deep in thought about Ace and our blonde waitress when I hear someone talking to me. I pull myself out of my thoughts and look up over my menu. Once I my gaze locked onto Roman's I froze. Panic setting in, and I glance to the bathrooms. Where the fuck is Ace when I need him. I go too slowly back away from the table to make a run for it. But I run into something. "Not so fast Layla. Don't you want to chat and catch up. It's been a while since we've talked." Leah says, standing directly behind me. Fuck! This was not part of our plan! She is using her fake friend's voice, and it cuts me a little deeper now that I know the truth of everything. "How about it Layla, let's go for a walk." Roman says.

Leah, not missing a beat, grabs my arm and pulls me from my seat. She circles her arm through mine to make it look like a friendly encounter. Roman stands and follows behind me as Leah pulls me away from the Café area. I look back and make eye contact with the blonde who was our waitress. I give her a panicked look, and her eyes go wide. She heads to the men's bathroom. I assume she was watching Ace as well. "Oh, don't worry about him; I left him a note." Roman says nonchalantly. "Such a little whore these days. Huh, Layla?" Leah says spitting a bit of venom in her words. "You guys won't get away with this." I try to sound strong, but my resolve is breaking. "Oh, naïve Layla. We already have." Leah says in an overly sweet voice. I hear a commotion behind us and see Ace barreling towards us. "Ace!!" I scream. But before he can get close enough to help, I am being shoved into a car. They speed away and out of sight. "Damn it!" I yell. I hear Roman laughing. Yeah, because kidnapping someone is a funny thing. "Fucking Psycho's. The fucking both of you!" I scream at them. They probably want me to cry and play the fucking victim. But I am done with that shit. "That's bold, don't you think? Calling us names. Could end up getting yourself hurt Layla." Leah says as she slaps me hard across the face. Fuck that hurt. But I don't dare let her know that. I just glar

ed up at her and spit the blood in my mouth on the seat beside me. "You'll pay for that." I say menacingly. She isn't even phased. Just turns back to face-front in her seat. We stop outside of town at what looks to be an abandoned gas station. This should be sanitary. Roman gets out, opens my door and yanks me out of the car by my hair. That definitely caused tears.

Trying to hold my own or not, that fucking hurt, man. I am drug inside and tied to a chair in the middle of the room. I see a mattress behind me in the corner and try not to shudder. I'll be okay. At least that's what I'm going to keep reminding myself until help arrives. I hope. "So, Layla, now that we have you all to ourselves. We can take our time. You know, reunite. Or, we could just start where we left off." Roman's eyes spark with heat as they shift between me and the mattress on the floor. I inwardly withdraw and curl up in a ball. But on the outside, I just smile and shake my head. "You've lost the battle Roman. There isn't anything about me to deflower anymore. You lost your chance! Sorry." I say, shrugging the best I can. His face morphs into something between rage and disgust. "You fucking whore." He yells at me and punches me so hard that the chair topples to the floor. My eyes are hazy, like I am trying to pass out. But not this time. I will myself stay alert. "Roman, she is toying with you. I've been close to her for a long enough time to know her. She wouldn't give it up so easily. Especially to a guy she just met a week ago." I can hear the disdain in her voice as she talks bout being my friend. "You aren't a fucking friend, and you don't know me." I say as I spit new blood across the floor. I know I shouldn't be pissing them off. But damn it, I am tired of this shit. After a few cuss words and a conversation in the back, Leah comes out and picks me and my chair back up. "Shut your mouth and behave. Or I'll let him have you, virgin or not." Leah spits in my face.

ACE

"Don't worry Cameron, I've got eyes on her." I say, trying to keep him calm. What I didn't tell him were the hits she had taken. But I can see her will to fight, and right before the hits, I see her talking. She is likely spouting off. God, I wish she wouldn't do that. I followed them out of town to this abandoned gas station. Johnny boy came to his word

when he gave us the heads up on this place earlier this morning. So even if I had lost them on the road, we would still have found her. I'm waiting on backup. But we are also a good 30 minutes out of town. Opposite the side of town, my clubhouse is on. This happened a lot sooner than I anticipated. Our plan was to use Layla as bait. But we would have had it set up as a trap for them to walk into, and not our girl being in actual danger. I'm so pissed right now, and I checked our surroundings before I ever decided to go ahead and use the restroom. This should never have happened. I promised I wouldn't let anything happen to her. Damn it! We should have been ready for it. But we weren't set up and ready for it, and it's all my fucking fault. It's going to take my people at least forty-five minutes to an hour to get here. I see the girl come out from the back and pick Layla up off the floor. She says something and then walks out. Layla rests her head on the back of the chair. I'm praying she doesn't fall asleep because that hit he landed could have easily given her a concussion. As long as they don't try anything too bad before my backup arrives, we should be fine. But I can see a glimpse of what looks like a mattress on the floor. From my point of view, it's difficult to tell. But since that is what they wanted her for, I presume that is what it is. I see movement and catch a glimpse of the prick Roman. He is circling Layla like prey. She keeps her face to the ceiling, ignoring him. Fuck, she is trying to be tough and is going to get herself hurt more. I know they are both carrying weapons, which is why I haven't tried anything. I don't know the layout of this building, and they could have anything stashed inside for protection. It's clear these two are the smart ones in their friend group. They have clearly thought this out so far. So I don't want to go in, just to get us both killed in the end for being ill-prepared.

LAYLA

I have my eyes closed, but my head is back facing the ceiling. Roman doesn't say anything as he enters the room. But I know it's him; the gross cologne he uses is making my stomach turn. I don't move, but I hear him circling me. Like prey, he is just waiting to pounce on me. It's nerve-wracking, and I know that's why he is doing it. Just to get under my skin. But I don't move, not a muscle. I hear him stop, and he is in front me. "I know you are not passed out or asleep. So why don't you sit up straight so we can talk." The tone of his voice is neutral. I slowly lower my head. Due to the throbbing pain of the hit he landed, moving makes me want to puke. Eventually, my head faces forward, and I open my eyes. Standing there with his arms crossed over his chest, Roman looks deadly. I'm not sure why I never saw any of this before. Him, Leah. How did I not see it when now it's all I see. I stare off behind him out the window. Almost in a daze. Yep, I'm concussed! Roman slowly approaches me. Kneeling in front of me, he reaches forward, and I try to recoil from his hand, but I can't move because I am stuck to this stupid chair. He grabs my shirt and rips it off right down the middle. I gasp in surprise but school my features quickly. "You have changed haven't you? Were did my meek little Layla go?" Roman asks with a glint of mischief showing through. "She found out she was being hunted and lied to. Taken advantage of. She isn't here anymore." I say through clenched teeth. "That's alright cupcake, I'll break you." He gives me what I think is supposed to be a smile. But whatever it is looked pure evil. I try my best not to look afraid, but I don't think it's working. As he watches me, his smile only grows. Untying me from the chair, my worst fear comes true. He drags me over to the mattress on the floor and throws me down onto it. He tries to descend down onto me, but I lose it and start kicking and hitting *him. He is even more pissed now. But at least I'm not the only one bleeding. "You fucking bitch!" he says before knocking me unconscious. When I come to, I'm still on the mattress, but now I've been tied down to it. I panic and start trying to get free. Though all I'm doing is hurting myself. These ropes are so tight I'm just causing rope burn, and it's starting to bleed. Wincing in pain, I give up before I hurt myself more. I note that I haven't seen Leah in a while and wonder if she left. I can see Roman across the room, looking out a window. Once I stopped struggling, he turned to me. "It's no use, Layla. You are not getting out of this, and no one is coming to save you. Mine as well, just give me what I want. Hell, you may even enjoy it." He says, winking at me. I involuntarily gag. His eyes go fierce, and he drops to the mattress, straddling me. "Why do you intend on pissing me off so much? Huh. I could have been nice and maybe helped you out to. But now all I'm going to do is take what I want from you. And I am going to make sure it hurts. You'll never forget me then, will you, cupcake. Maybe even scar up this pretty body of yours. Then no one will ever want you." He says the last part as he lightly slides the edge of a large knife from between my breasts all the way down my stomach. There is no hiding my terror now. He digs the knife just deep enough to cut through the fabric of my bra, cutting it in half. I am now bare to him."You know, Layla I did like you, we had so many things in common. But you see, I can't stand aside and let you get away with humiliating Johnny the way you did. So, unfortunately for you, it's time to pay up on that." Fumbling with my pants button and zipper, Roman gets mad and just rips my pants off of me, and I'm left in my underwear. I hear a loud crash and see Ace stand up from the floor. Oh, thank God! Relief washes over me. "Ace!" I scream. He does a quick look at the room. But he manages to dodge and get a hit in on Roman as he rushes toward him with the knife. Roman lands with a thud and stays there. Ace rushes over to me. Starting to untie me when a* gunshot rings through the building. "Don't worry, they're coming." Ace whispers to me before he falls to the ground. "No! Ace!" I am hysterical now. Tears are streaking my face and mixing with the now-dried blood. "Oh, I'm sorry was he important to you?" I look up to see Leah holding the gun that just shot Ace. "Get up!" She says, kicking Roman. "If he found us, the others aren't far behind. Do what we intended so we can go." She spits at him. Roman stands, coming back to me. I hear Ace groan as Roman kicks him out of the way. Well, at least he isn't dead. Or at least not yet. Roman wastes no time getting rid of my panties. I'm naked, tied down, and helpless. With one hand, he roughly grabs my breast and squeezes. I yelp at the pain and try to wiggle free. His other hand stops me dead as he cups my nether region. Taking his dirty fucking fingers, he slides them through my pussy. "Awe I'm disappointed, I must not have had enough foreplay to get you wet for me. Don't worry I'll fix it." Roman says, taking a finger and shoving it inside me. I gasp and start crying at the unwanted intrusion. "I'd be surprised if you aren't a virgin anymore girl. Your fucking tight as hell." He says smiling. "I fucking told you she was lying earlier." Leah says from behind him. "Ace!" I whimper, trying to plead. "he can't help you now." Roman says, starting to take his pants off. That's when I heard it. Motorcycles. There are so many it just sounds like a loud, continuous roar coming from outside. The men circle the building on ir bikes, making themselves known everywhere. They park surrounding the whole building. I hear a shot go off, and Leah is no longer standing. Roman is still on the floor with us, so he can't be seen through the window. Though I can see panic and fury in his eyes as he just watched Leah go down. My guys didn't come here to fight; they came to dominate. Untying me from the mattress, he hauls me up off the floor by my hair. Using me as a human target. I'm still naked, by the way. I can see all of Ace's guy's guns pulled, ready for him to fuck up and make a wrong move. All a sudden I'm jerked backwards and onto the wood floor. When I opened my eyes, the one person I wanted to see was right there. "Cameron!" With Roman out cold, he has let go of my hair. The bikers all ascend into the building, were they go to Ace. One hands Cameron a blanket. "Let's get you decent, baby girl." He says, scooping me off the floor and wrapping me in the blanket. "Ace!" I whisper to him. His eyes fly across the room till they land on Ace's figure on the floor. "Update," he calls out to the men around Ace. "Bullet went deep. He has lost a lot of blood. We need to get back to the house and get this bullet out." Someone answers. "Bring him into my car. I'll drive. And someone, please clean up this mess. He looks at me. Then looks over at Roman, who is starting to come to. In this moment Cameron does something I never thought he would do. He hands me the gun he used to knock Roman unconscious. Roman groans and tries to stand. Cameron pushes him back to the ground. Everyone is watching me. Wondering if I'm going to do it. Cameron has left the decision up to me. "What are you going to do Layla, shoot me?" There is amusement in his voice, like a challenge. But after everything he has done, I look away from him, feeling overwhelmed. Cameron sets me on my feet as people are carrying Ace to the car. "I fucking thought not." Roman says, and without hesitation, I raise the gun and pull the trigger. I'm shaking, but I hand the gun back to Cameron and walk out to the car. I hear Cameron give a few more orders before we are all in the car and rushing to the clubhouse to save Ace.

EPILOGUE

1 Year Later

LAYLA

Snuggled into the couch, I rub my hand down my belly. It's starting to stick out just a bit. Three months along, just getting over the morning sickness, ugh. I am just enjoying watching Cameron and I's little girl crawl around on the floor playing with her uncle Ace. I owe him everything. He almost died that night. Took a lot of recovery for him to be back to his old ways. Cameron asked me to marry him that night. I guess the thought of losing me was too much for him. Then, we found out two weeks later that I was pregnant. Johnny kept his end of the deal and made everything right with the college. So, I have gone back online for now so I can take care of our kids. Once I need hands-on classes, I will start back on campus. Cameron sold his house, and we bought one out of town closer to Ace's clubhouse. It has more rooms and more yard. Mrs. Magnolia stays with us a lot. She loves spending time with her granddaughter, and I appreciate the help. Especially now that we are expecting again.

THE END

www.ingramcontent.com/pod-product-compliance
Lightning Source LLC
Chambersburg PA
CBHW070335130626
46556CB00007B/2873